I

Readers sound off on
RICK STEELE: Squid Hunter:

"Yea, buy this book 'cause Greg needs the money for the vig on his loan." *Vinnie (no last name)*

"So he wrote a book, big deal. When's he gonna pick up around his place and mow the yard?" *Mrs. Nusbaum, Greg's neighbor.*

"Wow, he really wrote a book? I mean, he told us he was like a writer and stuff. Who knew? He was always a good tipper." *Samantha Suede at the Boom-Boom Club.*

"We cannot comment at this time and the restraining order is still in place." *Famous Australian actress' legal counsel.*

RICK STEELE:
Squid Hunter

Greg Causey

Cover by Jennifer Labelle

Copyright © 2015 Greg Causey

ISBN 978-1-939010-72-8

Published by Romance Divine LLC

A Note from the Author

Squids are real. And they are dangerous. *Very* dangerous. If you see a squid, run away. Wave your arms to warn others. Shout, "Squids! The Squids are here!" Notify the authorities. Find a safe place to hide until help arrives. Good places to hide are Gun Shops and Chain Saw stores. Bad places to hide are Fish Markets and Live Bait Shops. Do NOT play the "Hey Look at Me, I'm a Fish" game.

Acknowledgements

I would be remiss if I did not acknowledge those who inspired me during the writing of RICK STEELE: Squid Hunter. Joel, Tom and Crow from MST3000. Eric Idle, John Cleese, Michael Palin and the rest of the Monty Python troupe. Nigel Tufnel. The people at the SyFy Channel and Asylum Films. Craig Stevens and Lola Albright. Saturday Night Live. The History Channel, Discovery Channel and Animal Planet. Jeremy Wade and River Monsters. John Banner. Werner Klemperer. James Doohan. Danny Trejo.

Thanks to Joan and Kellie for reading the book and giving me feedback. Kudos to Jennifer Labelle for doing the cover for this book and for *Rick Steele versus the Mongolian Death Python*.

Introduction

I freely admit to a guilty pleasure: bad sci-fi and monster movies. From the days of *Mystery Science Theater 3000*, to those who fondly remember *that*, to the more modern fare found on Saturdays on the Sy-Fy Channel I am enamored with creatures who seek to wreak havoc on mankind: Sharktopus, Chupacabra, Mega Sharks, Giant Octopus, Giant Gila Monsters, Mega Piranha, DinoCroc, Supergator, Giant Leeches, Giant Pythons, Boas, or Anacondas and the rest garner my rapt attention and viewing time.

Lest the reader think I am uncultured, I will also admit that when my wife and I lived in California we attended and were patrons of the Oregon Shakespeare Festival in Ashland. When we lived in Europe we visited the great museums and cathedrals: The Louvre, The Hermitage, The Galleria de Academia, The Uffizi, Victoria and Albert and many, many others.

But I *do* love my "B" movie sci-fi. I also have a passion and curiosity about Cephalopods. If there is a Discovery Channel or Animal Planet Channel documentary about the squid or octopus you can bet I will be watching.

As a publisher, when my authors sent in a manuscript I would often reply, "Wow, wouldn't it be great if the hero could save the heroine's baby from the Giant Squid people?" The answer was always, "No, Greg, not in my book! Write your own book if you want something with a Giant Squid."

So… Based on my love of bad sci-fi, and my innate interest in squids, I give you *RICK STEELE: Squid Hunter*.

Greg Causey 2015

For Joan, who has patiently sat through too many bad Sci-Fi monster movies with me.

I LOVE YOU.

Greg

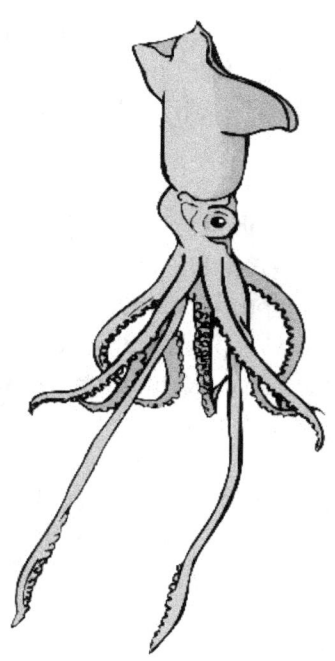

RICK STEELE:
Squid Hunter

Greg Causey

PROLOGUE

The Year of Our Lord 1492

The four ships rolled lazily on the water, the stillness of the night broken only by the creaking of wood and ropes. Swaying lanterns marked the position of each ship against the night sky.

"Hey, Esteban," a grizzled sailor on the *Niña* called across the water to the man on watch on the *Pinta*. "Maybe we land soon, find some *mujeres, si?*"

Esteban waved back, land and women would be a welcome change from the long voyage to who knew where.

Both men turned their gaze back to the west, looking over the bows of their ships. They'd sailed for weeks since leaving *Palos de la Frontera*, trusting in their leader, 'Admiral of the Ocean Sea', Christopher Columbus to lead them on an adventure…a new route to the Far East.

On his flagship, the *Santa Maria*, Christopher Columbus paced the deck, unable to sleep. He'd been confident of finding a new path to China, but his ability to energize his men was beginning to wane. They were restless. And scared.

Esteban looked to his right and back toward the stern, to the fourth ship of the expedition, the *El Gato Negro*, which sailed behind the other three. The lantern on the ship pitched with the rolling of the sea and in the moonlight he saw two figures moving on the deck. The night was quiet, save for the lapping of the waves and the creaking of the boats. He turned his gaze back to the west, a sudden chill making him shiver and he absently made the sign of the cross. He crinkled his nose; the smell of sea, salt and sweat was now abetted with something more acrid. Something... Foreign.

Behind him he now heard voices and turned back again to see men flooding the deck of the *El Gato Negro*, staring down at the water. The once tranquil water now seemed to boil against the sides of the ship. Flashes of red and white bloomed in the water, hundreds of bursts of light.

Two huge tentacles exploded from the water, wrapping around the hull of the *El Gato Negro*. By now, all eyes from the crews of the *Niña, Pinta* and *Santa Maria* were focused on the horror visited on their fellow seamen. Men muttered *Madre de Dios* and crossed themselves.

"To arms," Columbus cried out, a command echoed on the other two ships. Men scurried to grab swords and clubs.

An explosion ripped through the night, momentarily drowning out the screams of the sailors, as the keel of the *El Gato Negro* snapped, broken like a twig under the power of the unseen sea monster. The once-proud ship snapped in two. Men spilled into the sea. Others clutched onto pieces of the ship, climbing higher on the masts as the ship slowly settled into the water.

The men in the water struggled frantically to grab onto barrels or pieces of wood, but squids, the size of grown men, attacked them, dragging them under until their screams were silenced by the deep.

As quickly as it began, it was over. Not a soul from the *El Gato Negro* was left alive. The sea was calm again, bits of wood floating on the surface, the only sign that a proud ship, and its crew, had once been there.

The men on the other three ships kept a nervous watch, expecting another attack at any moment, but there was only silence as the little fleet sailed on.

Columbus turned to the hooded cleric beside him, the spiritual advisor and chronicler of the voyage. "Brother Maynard, the count shall be three," Columbus looked at his trio of ships remaining, his shoulders fell, "and three shall be the count. Four is right out."

Brother Maynard nodded.

"You must swear all the men," Columbus gazed at his three remaining ships, "to silence. On pain of eternal damnation and excommunication, no one must ever speak of this."

Later that night, by the flicker of a small candle, Brother Maynard unrolled a leather scroll and inked his quill: 'Devils from the sea…'

ONE

2015...Tuesday

The fog crept in from the bay, snaking its way along the back streets and curling like tentacles around lampposts. Off in the distance Rick Steele heard the mournful clanging of a harbor buoy. From down the alley came the sounds of a piano and the clatter of glasses as Sam, the bartender, threw another stack of empties outside the back door of his jazz club, *Pop's*. He crouched down, his hand disappearing into the damp mist, his fingers feeling the slime on the pavement. He brought the finger to his nose and detected the faint aroma of ammonia. Rick Steele narrowed his dark eyes as he peered into the gloom. Further down the alley the mist rose and fell, eerie fingers wafting into the damp night. A faint rustling and scraping noise echoed between the brick buildings and faded away. He nodded to his sidekick across the street, they had a trail.

He stood, opening his long duster coat and pulling the right side past the Ruger 44 Magnum on his right hip. For a second he was silent and still, taking in all around him. He sniffed at the air: a mixture of salt sea breeze, tobacco, stale cabbage from Mr. Wong's Deli... And Squid. He'd been tracking this one for three days, and was getting close. *You slipped up by going for the fish market at closing time. And tonight you'll pay.*

RICK STEELE: Squid Hunter

He moved purposefully down the alley, not in a rush, but confident, his trusty sidekick Choo making his way up the opposite side of the alley. His eyes watched for tell-tale disturbances in the fog, his ears were focused on the slapping sounds of tentacles on the alley's bricks, and the scent of ammonia was in the air, stronger now. *More difficult isn't it, on land? The vaunted squid mobility is useless out of water. Should've stayed in your domain. Come to mine—and you die.*

A blinking neon sign bloomed through the fog and mist: ROOMS: NIGHT or WEEKLY. He saw the viscous trail as it led to the door. He walked in. The desk clerk was half asleep as two elderly borders watched an old black and white TV in the corner. Rick rapped his fist on the counter, bringing the clerk out of his stupor.

"Wh-what? Uh… Need a room, Mister?" He looked at the tall stranger and the Oriental man next to him.

Rick saw the slime trail lead to the stairs. "Anybody come in and out of here within the last few minutes?"

"Huh? Uh, I-I dunno. You a cop or somethin'?"

"Somethin'." Rick drew his revolver and followed the squid sign up the stairs and down the third floor hall. *Must be your first time on land, bad move to put yourself on the third floor with no way out*. He reached into his coat and pulled out a small spray bottle, bending over to spray a fine mist under the door and into the room. The fishy smell of Cod filled the hallway and Rick heard excited rustling on the other side of the door. He watched as the door handle began to turn and then discharged four rounds through the door. The gunshots echoed down the hall and broke the stillness of the night.

Without waiting, Rick pulled the 9 MM Glock 19

from the holster at the small of his back and kicked the door open. The squid, one of the largest Humboldts he'd ever seen, was thrashing about the room and violently changing colors.

The squid backed up and stilled when Rick entered the room. Rick watched its funnel distend and heard a slight whooshing sound. A black substance flowed down the squid's body.

Choo entered behind Rick, taking a position off to the side to black any exit by their quarry.

Rick laughed, "Doesn't work so good out of water does it?"

Tentacles flapped on the cheap carpet of the hotel room. The squid turned its body to focus its large eye on Rick. The Chromatophores on its body blinked out a psychedelic pattern of different colored hues.

"Go ahead and flash, you're all alone here, no killer-squid colleagues to bail out your Cephalopod ass. Blink out your last squid goodbye." Rick held the Ruger in his right hand and the Glock in his left, as he kicked the door behind him closed. He turned to Choo, "Get some video for the Professor."

The squid moved across the floor, slowly, pulling itself forward on its arms, the longer and wicked feeding tentacles ripping up the carpet in front of it.

Choo pulled out a small camera and began filming.

"Out of water, bad mistake," Rick maintained his distance, letting the squid tire itself out. "Live fast, die young, isn't that the squid morphology? Looks like you'll be meeting your end a bit sooner my boneless friend."

The squid lashed out with a tentacle, missing Rick, but cutting a velvet bullfighter painting on the wall nearly in half.

"Now that's a damn shame," Rick growled. "You'll die for being a squid. And for crimes against the art community."

The squid charged, using its eight arms to thrust itself up from the carpet and toward Rick, its tentacles making a hissing sound as they cut through the air. Rick dodged one of the tentacles, but the other hit his arm, slashing his well-worn and cherished leather jacket.

The squid lashed out at Choo, but the nimble Korean threw the camera into the air with his left hand and ducked low, simultaneously pulling a machete from the scabbard on his back with his right hand and severing a tentacle in one savage blow. As he rose he slipped the machete back into the scabbard and caught the camera before it hit the floor.

"Nice," Rick said, "maybe I should call you Machete."

Choo gave a toothy grin, "Too late, Boss."

The squid charged Rick and the Ruger roared twice, the heavy slugs throwing the squid back, the holes they created releasing more of the pungent ammonia smell into the room. The squid floundered, weakened now, but still dangerous with the long tentacles.

Rick lifted the Glock and aimed for the center of the squid body. "Calamari time, baby." Eight nine-millimeter bullets nearly cut the squid in half at the posterior surface.

The squid's tentacles and arms thrashed as it collapsed to the floor of the cheap flop-house room. Black liquid oozed from the squid's wounds and pooled on the floor.

"Hey there, what the hell—" the desk clerk barged

into the room and then staggered back at the sight of Rick Steele, a gun in each hand, standing over the body of a large Humboldt squid. "What'd you do, Mister? And what the hell is that," he pointed a shaking finger, "that thing?"

Elderly occupants poked their heads around the door, murmuring among themselves.

Steele turned, holstering his weapons. "You never saw *that* come in here?"

"Hell no, ain't allowed, not never. Management don't allow no pets, or no cookin' neither. No way." He looked at the ripped carpet and the shredded velvet bullfighter painting, "Hey! Who's gonna pay for that?"

Steele's gray eyes glared and the desk clerk backed away. "Take it up with the City Boarding Commission. Explain to them why you're renting rooms to squids."

"Didn't never. No, never said I did."

Steele ignored the desk clerk and walked to the squid. He drew a large hunting knife from the sheath on his belt and knelt near the squid. The onlookers gasped as he cut away parts of the squid, putting the pieces in plastic bags or small bottles.

Choo took several pictures and sealed up the severed tentacle in a plastic bag.

"What're you gonna do with that thing?"

"Me?" Rick turned to face the clerk. "Nothing, I eighty-sixed it, so now it's your problem. I suggest you get rid of it. Before it stinks up this dive any worse." He turned and walked from the room, the hallway of disheveled gawkers parting like the Red Sea to let him pass.

*****

Steele plopped onto the barstool as Sam slid a shot in front of him and Choo.

"Bad one?" Sam wiped the bar with a grimy white rag.

"Bad enough, and further inland than I've seen." Steele tossed back the drink. "Third-floor flop house down on Bleaker. Big one." He turned to watch the stage, "Bad tempered son-of-a-bitch too."

Choo downed his drink. "Hey, Boss, I go now, take samples and video to Professor. Okay?"

Rick nodded, "I'll be there in a while."

Sam refilled Steele's glass, "This one's the good stuff. On me."

Steele nodded, his gaze focused on Lola. The sultry songbird was belting out a torch song, her voluptuous curves a sensuous vision through the club's dim light and haze of smoke. The quartet, led by Clifford the pianist, churned out a mournful tune as Lola Fontaine sang about lost love.

"Ya think we have anything to worry about?" Sam's question interrupted Steele's thoughts.

"Don't know. My advice is to be careful. All I know for now is that it's not over, not by a long shot." He saw the band end its set and Lola walk from the stage."

"Rick Steele," Lola's black-gloved hand picked up the Champagne cocktail Sam placed in front of her. She brought the drink to her ruby-red lips, her smoky eyes staring over the glass at Rick, "Been wondering when I'd see you in here again."

Rick's eyes followed as Lola slid her form onto a barstool. The long beaded gown clung to her every curve, a long slit exposing her long leg and high heel. His eyes finally rested on her ample cleavage, revealed by the low cut dress. "Been busy."

Her tongue flicked the traces of Champagne from her lips as her gloved hand pushed away his coat and stroked the long barrel of his Ruger revolver. "Hunting those… Things?"

His silence and the look in his eyes when he threw back his next drink told her the answer was 'yes'. "I'd like to stay, but I have to see someone right now."

She batted her long black lashes, "You know where to find me."

TWO

The convoy of black SUV's made its way along the deserted road. The three vehicles traveled up to a small building. A high fence, topped with razor wire, extended as far as the eye could see. Cameras along the perimeter moved slowly and ominously. Watching…

The SUVs stopped at a gate near the small building. They were quickly surrounded by teams of men in camouflaged uniforms, assault weapons at the ready. One team of men circled the vehicles with dogs; another ran mirrors under the vehicles while yet another team checked the credentials of the occupants.

There was no indication *where* they were. The signage at the building and all along the fence was the standard bureaucratic security-speak:

`No Trespassing. No Admittance Without Authorization. Use of Deadly Force Authorized`.

If one looked close enough they would have identified the guard uniforms as U.S. Marine Corps, yet there was nothing to identify the nature of the secured facility.

One of the guards passed the ID's back to the individuals in the second SUV, snapped to attention with a salute and waved the vehicles through.

The caravan in black moved on, down the deserted road and up over a small ridge. In the distance, the setting sun painted orange streaks across the horizon. The blue Pacific Ocean stretched as far as the eye could see. The coastline to the north and south was deserted. Further down the road was a cluster of buildings and a small, but high-tech dock, with three ships berthed.

The buildings came into focus as the vehicles neared. They were stark and windowless, a uniform gray color with no markings other than 1, 2, 3, etc.

More guards appeared as the vehicles parked in front of building number two. The SUV occupants assembled in front of the door as their credentials were checked a second time. Thoroughly vetted, they now entered.

A Marine guard led the group down a hallway. They passed doors shut and locked with combination locks and biometric identification systems.

The throng moved silently, save for the clop of boots, men's expensive Italian loafers and a woman's high-heeled pumps.

The guard ushered them through a doorway, shutting the door behind them and standing guard.

"Madame Secretary," a three-star Admiral moved forward to greet the visitors. "We're honored to have you here. I've prepared—"

"Cut the bullshit, Curt. I'm not here for a fifty-slide dog and pony show. I want to know *why* our project went off the reservation and what *you* are doing about it. I can't sit on this forever, people are going to find out; fishermen and boaters are going missing, the fishing fleet catch is down."

Admiral Seez scowled. *Women don't belong on ships or in positions of power*. "We're tracking it, Madame Secretary, and we are prepping one of our ships to re-capture it and bring it back in."

Madame Secretary Anita Mann hardly seemed mollified. She stood, her arms crossed, one foot rocking slowly on its designer stiletto heel. "*What* went wrong? Can we contain and fix this?"

Admiral Seez took a step back. "We were running the first set of sea trials outside the holding pen. We had a power failure and the specimen stopped responding to our wireless neural network. We lost control and weren't able to reestablish." He gestured to the tall, thin man next to him, "I'll allow Dr. Theerie to explain the technical details."

A tall, austere man stepped forward. He was thin, bald and with piercing black eyes. His white lab coat was immaculate, without a wrinkle. "Our Giant Squid specimen, number seventeen, has a locator beacon embedded. We should be able to track its location unless it goes into the Abyssalpelagic zone."

Secretary Mann sighed, *science shit*, "Which is?"

"Approximately four thousand meters deep."

Her eyes widened as she did a rough math calculation. "Twelve thousand feet? Can squids *go* that deep?"

Dr. Theerie grimaced. "It's likely, there is still much unknown about these creatures."

She rolled her eyes. "So… You *think* you know

where it is and you *hope* to get it back? What—Happened?"

Dr. Theerie shifted on his feet. "As I said, there is still much we do not know. This program is in its infancy. The science—"

"This is what we get after almost a billion dollars of my money?" The speaker was an older, gray-haired man in an expensive suit.

"Not to mention significant black budget resources," Secretary Mann added.

"We *have* made progress," the Admiral interjected.

"*Progress* doesn't pay the bills," Secretary Mann retorted, "*results* do. You promised me a super-intelligent squid with superior strength, a 21st century Battle Squid, able to work at depth to attack enemy submarines and ocean-floor listening networks, able to attack enemy surface ships. Even able to attack and take enemy beachheads." She paused to gaze around her audience. "And what we *have*… Is a rogue squid, attacking boats and fishermen, playing havoc with the coastal fishing industry and threatening to put all of us in the newspaper and on the six o'clock news."

The group fell silent. Admiral Seez's lips were firm, his teeth grinding. He didn't like being dressed-down by a woman, a *political appointee.*

Dr. Theerie broke the silence. "Madame Secretary, we *have* made progress. The specimen is smarter and stronger, more aggressive. We merely need to perfect our neural-pathway control elements software interface to create your first-generation Archetuthis Battle Squid." He extended a conciliatory hand, "Please, Madame Secretary, allow me to show you some of the things we have been able to accomplish."

Secretary nodded, and allowed her group to be led to another part of the laboratory complex.

"Is that—Thing?—Walking?" Madame Secretary took a step back as she watched a six-foot Humboldt squid move, on its squid arms, across the cement floor of its enclosure.

Dr. Theerie beamed with pride. "It is, after a fashion, an elemental form of locomotion out of water." He paused, "All living creatures have a carbon base. We've created a way for these creatures to synthesize their own carbon to create a simple carbon fiber exoskeleton. One that supports their weight out of water, where they would normally depend on buoyancy. As you know, carbon fiber can be stronger and lighter than steel."

Secretary Mann nodded, "I *am* impressed."

Dr. Theerie continued. "Imagine, thousands, hundreds of thousands, of six-to-seven-foot Humboldt squids storming a beach, overrunning defenses, clearing the way for your troops." His lips formed a cruel smile, "No need to worry about casualties and no enemy could survive against such an onslaught."

She turned to Admiral Seez, "Okay, you bought yourself some time. But find this renegade Giant Squid and get it under control."

Admiral Seez saluted, "Yes, Ma'am."

*****

Admiral Seez opened his desk drawer and removed a bottle of Scotch, filling two glasses and passing one across his desk to Dr. Theerie. "We still have time to fix this."

Dr. Theerie took a drink. "It's not going to be easy. It took five attempts to finally catch an Archetuthis and implant the neural and genetic hardware on a living sample. And now... Sample seventeen is gone. It's stronger and smarter now, thanks to us. It won't be easy to capture it a second time."

Admiral Seez drained his glass and filled it a second time. "What about specimen number twenty; do we tell our vaunted Madame Secretary about *that* one?"

Dr. Theerie stared across the Admiral's office at pictures of ships on the wall. "That... Would be unwise. We don't yet know the full capabilities of that one. If we can recapture number seventeen, perhaps we can use it to help us find and control number twenty." He looked at Admiral Seez, "It might also be best if she doesn't know about the Humboldt squids that escaped as well. They will die soon; it's doubtful they will be able to breed and pass along any of their enhanced genetics."

The Admiral slammed his empty glass on his desk. "My career is in danger of being ruined by a bunch of drugged-up, high-tech, cyber calamari."

*****

Madame Secretary turned to the billionaire beside her. "Your thoughts, Herr Geld? You're funding a large part of this project."

He gazed out the tinted window, "Most new endeavors experience stages of development, set-backs, triumphs. This is an ambitious melding of biology and technology." He tented his hands, "The long-term technological spinoffs can mean billions."

"Squids," Madame Secretary huffed, "I mean…"

Herr Geld raised his hand. "The legend of the Kraken goes back centuries, millennia. Even Columbus…" He fell silent. "The Giant Squid *is* real. Who is to say *we* cannot create the Kraken and bring the myth to life?"

THREE

Rick Steele pulled his car in front of the non-descript building and knocked on the heavy steel door, lifting his chin to peer in the camera mounted above. He waited and heard the metallic sound of a magnetic lock releasing and entered the building.

His heavy boots echoed down the bare concrete walls of the corridor. At the end was another steel door and camera, where Rick repeated the same procedure, finally gaining access to the professor's laboratory.

"Rick!" Professor Von Hell-Sink lumbered forth. He was a portly man in a white lab coat, his wild shock of gray hair matched by the same gray and bushy eyebrows. His bright blue eyes twinkled behind small, round eye glasses. "These samples are most fascinating. Tell me about the creature." His voice had an Eastern-European accent, but held excitement about Rick's latest encounter.

"You were right. They are moving inland and this one displayed no fear of humans at all. In fact, it was downright aggressive."

The professor held one of the jars up, squinting his eyes and peering at it through the light. "Yes, I feared as much. And I doubt we've seen the worst. They are probing, testing our weaknesses."

"You think we'll see more," Rick said as a statement of fact, not a question.

"Almost certainly," the professor shook his head, "and in more numbers. You'll probably see them more in groups, rather than the single one you killed tonight. Their advantages lie in their numbers and rapid life cycle." He turned to Rick, a worried look now painting the professor's face, "They must be stopped. And soon."

Rick shed his leather jacket, "I don't disagree, Professor," and dropped it over a chair. He removed his shoulder holster as well. His short-sleeved shirt revealed muscled arms, the forearms thick with sinewy tendons rippling along their length. His black hair framed a chiseled and handsome face, with piercing dark eyes and a stubble of beard that gave him a rugged and manly look. "Do you have any idea where they will strike next? Or even what the hell they're after? None of this makes any sense; all I know is that I have to kill them."

The professor placed his hand on Rick's shoulder, "You've had a heavy burden my boy. No one should have to endure the trials you've faced."

Rick simply shrugged. The Professor was like a father to him, the only who believed a young boy's tale of tragedy at sea. They'd all treated him like a panic-stricken survivor, the lone member of a family lost at sea, rescued after clinging to a Styrofoam beer cooler for three days. His account of the family's sailboat being attacked by a Giant Squid, the family horribly killed before his eyes was too impossible for anyone to believe. Doctors and psychologists treated the boy for stress and delusions brought on by the tragedy.

Only Professor-Doktor Von Hell-Sink believed him. He visited the young Rick one day, and listened intently to the boy's tale. It was the Professor who guided Rick on his quest, sent him to professionals in martial arts skills, weapons, and physical fitness, while also training him in biology. The Professor had seen the signs and knew what would be coming. There were creatures, known and unknown, in the animal kingdom that threatened the very existence of man. The Professor had turned Rick into his weapon to defeat the onslaught. He believed many creatures, mammals and cephalopods alike, could communicate, and that in their world the name, Rick Steele: Squid-Hunter, would be known—and feared.

"Herr Steele, I trust you have brought us something *interressant?*" The Professor's assistant, Helga *Grosse-Brust*, approached. Her blonde hair was pulled back tight to her skull, ending in a severe bun behind her head. A white lab coat hid her svelte Nordic frame, pulled taut over her large breasts, but even in her flat shoes she stood eye-to-eye with the tall and strapping Steele. Ice-blue eyes fixed on the squid-hunter and her lips, with just a hint of pink, pursed, "*Ja?*"

"Helga," the Professor held out the specimens, "we must start analyses of these right away. From what Rick tells me, this creature was quite different from the last ones."

She accepted the specimens, her mouth turning up just slightly with a demure, yet wicked, smile. "Of course, Professor, I do like to check out new… And exciting, specimens." She turned and walked away with a Teutonic precision, and Rick couldn't help but notice the undulations of her hips beneath the white lab coat.

"Rick, come, come here, look at this," the Professor ushered Rick to a nearby table where a large map full of notes lay. "I've been reading news reports, examining catch reports from fishing boats, and measuring water temperature and salinity. I'm starting to believe…"

*****

"So…you're saying some guy came in here, shot up a *sea monster*, cut pieces off and left?" Drop-dead gorgeous ace reporter Loida Enal turned slowly on the spike heel of her exquisite designer pump and surveyed the room. It still reeked of some kind of dead fish, with a distinct ammonia smell, and a large and bloody squid carcass took center place on the floor.

"That's right," the desk clerk nodded, "big guy, with lots of guns. A real dangerous type. Had some ornamental fella with him." He scratched his head, "Though I suppose women might call him good looking."

"Hell, Jackson," a large barefoot woman in a faded house dress cackled from the hallway, "I'd let that handsome stranger park his boots under my bed anytime."

Loida turned to her attention to the barrel-chested detective O'Bannion, pointing her microphone in his direction. "Detective, do you have any leads as to why this creature was here, or who the mysterious squid killers were?"

"We're interviewing witnesses and gathering evidence, but it's an ongoing case. I've got nothing for you right now. The Chief will brief the press later." He turned to talk to a uniformed officer.

Loida dropped the microphone to her side and tossed back a mane of brown hair that flowed over her creamy shoulders like lava. "Jaime, you getting all this?"

Her cameraman, Jaime Noslo, turned in place, the

large black video camera on his shoulder. "Yea, gettin' it all. You want to set up and do a spot and then we can do any other voice-overs back at the studio?" He stopped to get a close-up of the ripped velvet bullfighter painting and the shredded and stained carpet.

"Yes," she looked around and framed herself between the stained and torn floor, and the ripped painting, "let's try and get as much carnage as possible in the shot." She quickly brushed her hair and touched up her lips before taking her place in front of the dead squid.

She watched for the red light on the camera to illuminate. "This is Loida Enal reporting from the Dempsy Hotel on Bleaker Street where tonight a mysterious stranger supposedly killed a sea monster, what looks to be a squid of some sorts, in front of witnesses. Several shots were fired and the creature was killed. Then the stranger and his accomplice cut away several parts of the mysterious creature and took them with them when they left. Stay tuned for further developments as we have them. This is Loida Enal for El Segundo Cable Network News." She pulled the microphone across her neck to indicate she was through.

"You know," Jaime started packing up his camera kit, "this isn't the first one of these."

Loida's fiery black eyes fixed on her cameraman, "Really?"

"There's been a couple of reports, unverified, of some guy shooting up something like this," he gestured with his hand to the debris scattered around the room. "But they all took place near the water, Clark's Bay and Murphy's Point."

Loida shook her head slowly, the vague details

coming back, "Yea, I remember, thought it was college kids, or some drunk."

Jaime shrugged, "Maybe, maybe not."

FOUR

Only a mile off Murphy's Point the sea floor dropped into a dark abyss. Surface light faded away hundreds of feet above and only the bioluminescence of the indigenous inhabitants gave clue to the teeming and varied life below.

The Giant Squid hovered in the black stillness, its eight arms and two long feeding tentacles undulating seductively. Even in the blackness its giant eyes could see, and it surveyed its realm.

A marine biologist would have considered the sight the culmination of a lifetime of work, to see the incredible gathering of diverse aquatic life. Surrounding the Giant Squid were hundreds, perhaps thousands, as their numbers faded into the vast blackness of the sea, of Humboldt Squid, their bodies blinking a kaleidoscope of color as their chromatophores illuminated the waters around them.

The powerful Humboldts darted about the water and gradually, one-by-one, began to slowly circle the Giant Squid, their blinking chromatophore soon synching into reddish hues. The Giant Squid held court, its devoted minions, now thousands in number, circling and blinking. Vampire squid, their red eyes glowing like coals in the depths, moved up and down through the assembled squid throng, streaking like fireworks on a summer evening. Not since Riefenstahl's *Triumph of the Will* had there been such a display of ominous pageantry.

Below the melee a Colossal Squid, heavier than the

Giant Squid though not as long, floated in the depths. Suddenly, the feeding tentacles of the Giant Squid lashed out, attacking and pulling the Colossal Squid upwards. Before the prey could react the Humboldts were upon it, darting in and out, ripping away pieces of the Colossal Squid's flesh.

The Giant Squid released its grip on its prey and slowly sank away into the blackness of the abyssal depths. As it did so its giant eye watched the carnage above, as the Humboldts carried out their cannibalistic ritual on the now lifeless Colossal Squid. The army was assembled, the sacrifice made.

FIVE

"Looks rather benign to me," Loida's eyes scanned the sandy beach, bits of green seaweed and kelp glistening on the sand as the sun set in the distance, casting a reddish-orange hue to the scene.

"Well," Jaime gestured with his free hand, "this is it, Murphy's Point." He pointed to a spit of land projecting into the sea.

"Go ahead and get some background footage," Loida said. "I'm going to talk to some of the locals." She trudged off to the nearby dock, her expensive stilettos sinking into the sand.

Two grizzled fisherman, an old-timer and his younger first-mate were tying up their fishing boat as Loida approached.

"You just coming in?" Loida straightened her skirt and brushed back her hair as she approached.

A man with a weathered face and scruffy white beard turned to her, "Yep."

"Catch anything?" She gave her hair a sexy and subtle flip.

His eyes narrowed and his companion stopped to watch the exchange. "You with the government?"

She flashed her reporter's credentials and her most charming smile, "Loida Enal, with El Segundo Cable News."

"Mexican news now doin' fishin' reports?"

She ramped up the charm, putting one hand sexily on her hip and shrugged. "I heard there was an incident at the point a while back."

The other man spoke up, "Yea, damndest thing ever, this guy—" A glare from the old-timer cut him off.

Loida stood on her tiptoes to look down into the boat, "No fish on this trip?"

The old-timer turned to face the water and nodded, "If they're out there I woulda caught 'em."

"It's the squids," the younger crewman was again silenced by a withering look from his Captain.

"Squids?" Her reporter's instinct smelled a story.

The old-timer stepped off the dock and down into his boat. He pulled back a tarp on the deck to expose a dead seven-foot Humboldt squid.

Loida shrank back, "What the hell is *that*?"

The old-timer kicked at the lifeless squid. "Squid, Humboldt squid. And a damn big one by my experience."

She pointed a shaky finger at the carcass, "That's...*out there*?"

He dropped the tarp back over the dead squid, "There's hundreds, hell, maybe more." He pointed to his nets, "Why we can't get no fish. These things eat up everything in sight."

She took out her phone to take pictures, "Have they always been out there? Where did they come from?" Loida pointed to the covered body, "Can I get a picture of you and the squid? Oh, and your crew too?"

The old-timer sighed, "Reckon I don't see why not, ain't gonna be sellin' no fish today."

As he uncovered the squid Loida waved to get Jaime's attention.

Loida clicked away with her cellphone camera as the Captain and his mate posed for pictures with the squid. When Jaime arrived she convinced the men to do a video interview.

"This is Loida Enal from Murphy's Point. I'm investigating the sudden appearance of hoards of voracious squids and their impact on the fishing industry. With me is Captain John Hawk, who has fished this area for several years. Captain Hawk, do you know where these squids came from?"

"Well," he scratched his chin, "couldn't rightly say. Some scientists from the institute were here a while back, said that these squids mostly liked it around Mexico." He shrugged and nodded to the boat behind him, where the squid lay exposed for the video, "And now… Here they are."

Jaime panned down to get footage of the squid.

"And you say they are having a serious impact on the fishing in the area?" Loida held the microphone out to Captain Hawk.

"Damn straight. These things eat almost anything, hell, they'll even eat each other." He spat on the deck. "Mexicans call 'em Diablo Rojo, 'red devils', can't say as I disagree with that."

"Is anyone doing anything about them?" Loida continued.

"Them scientists from the institute up the coast, they been down here to study 'em." He snorted, "But that ain't helpin' us who got to fish for a living."

Loida turned to face Jaime, "This is Loida Enal, El Segundo Cable News, from Murphy's Point."

Jaime climbed down into the boat with the first mate

to get footage of the squid while Loida questioned Captain Hawk.

She nodded at the dead squid and then toward the ocean, "There's more of those out there? You've seen them?"

"Ocean's full of 'em. 'Specially at night." He wiped the back of his hand across his brow. "They come up from the depths to feed."

"Would you take us out there?" she asked. "Me and my cameraman? To film them?"

He laughed, "Ain't no place for a pretty thing like you. And it's dangerous. You fall over they could be on you. They come in groups." He sighed, "Fishin's dangerous enough as it is, the sea can be a cruel Mistress, but with those things out there…"

She twisted on the heel of her expensive pump, "So where are they? I mean out there?"

"Ain't hard to find, just go out there at night and shine a bright light in the water and hang a bait over the side." He shook his head, "They'll find you."

As Loida and Jaime walked back to the van she looked over her shoulder at the Captain and his mate as they secured their fishing boat. "Jaime, doesn't your cousin have a boat?

SIX

"Whooo!" Monica Grant, 'Mon' to her friends, screamed and nearly fell overboard as Brad pulled the sleek cabin cruiser into a sharp turn. She righted herself and tossed back her blonde hair, laughing and slurping down the Vodka that hadn't spilled from her glass.

"Go, Brad!" Jake Beaumont held aloft his beer, cheering his friend on. Behind him, his girlfriend, Lindsay, wrapped her arms around his waist, pressing her large breasts, barely constrained by the tiny bikini top, into his back.

"Awesome!" Lindsay screamed, her blonde hair flowing in the wind.

Brad backed off on the throttle, the bow of the sleek boat dropping slowly back into the water, the churning wake glowing white in the light of the full moon. The boat's powerful motor now idled with a muted rumble, accompanied by the slapping of the waves on the hull.

Mon stumbled over to Brad in her stiletto thongs, trying to maintain her balance on the pitching deck. "Geez, Brad, your Dad's boat rocks!" She stumbled forward into Brad's arms.

"I told you not to wear those shoes," Brad looked down at her feet.

She scrunched her eyes and peered down, "But they're like, really cute." She pouted.

"Whatever." Brad released Mon and watched her

walk to the stern, swaying her bikini-clad bottom and blowing him a kiss over her shoulder. She stretched out on the cushions.

Jake stood with one arm around Lindsay's waist and pointed with the other to the dim blinking lights off in the distance, "That's Murphy's Point."

"Wow, how far out are we?" Lindsay asked.

"'Bout two or three miles," Brad screwed the top off another beer and sat next to the supine Mon.

"Let's see if there's any fish!" Lindsay grabbed a powerful hand-held spotlight and turned it on, aiming the bright light into the murky depths.

"C'mon," Jake looked to see Brad and Mon making out on the cushions, and turned his gaze back to Lindsay. She was now leaning over the railing, her bottom waving as she played the light over the surface of the water. "Lindsay…"

"Hey! I think I see something." Lindsay waved Jake over.

The Humboldts moved up from the deep, hundreds of powerful squids, attracted first by the vibrations of the boat's motors and now by the bright light penetrating the surface of the water. As they ascended, the hull of the white boat came into view.

Further below them, the Giant Squid rose from the depths.

"Look," Lindsay waved the light over the water. "See, there's something down there, a bunch of big fish."

Jake shook his head, "Yea..." He peered into the water, "I'm not so sure."

The water around the boat came alive, as if boiling, and Lindsay jumped back, almost knocking Jake over. The spotlight dropped from her hand, sinking into the depths, the light still glowing as it faded away into the blackness.

Slapping sounds filled the night air, as if someone were hitting the hull of the boat with wet towels.

Brad broke his embrace with Mon and joined Jake and Lindsay as they peered at the spectacle in the water around them. The water roiled with the bodies of squids surfacing and then diving, while others seemed to attack the boat, slapping at it with their tentacles.

"What *are* those?" Lindsay screamed.

Jake shrugged, "I dunno, some kind of octopus or squid?"

Lindsay clutched Jake, wrapping her arms around him. "Let's go! Let's get out of here."

Brad nodded, "Yea, maybe we should..."

As suddenly as it started, the frantic explosion of the water stilled, the only sound now, the waves lapping against the hull.

Jake and Brad cautiously approached the boat's railing, looking over the side, and seeing nothing.

Jake shrugged, "Huh, must've gone. Maybe they were feeding on some fish or something?"

The Giant Squid's enormous eyes had the white hull of the boat in view. It's long and deadly feeding tentacles shot out, each one grabbing one side of the hull.

Jake and Brad jumped back as the ends of the tentacles curled over the side of the boat, slapping with a horrendous sound.

"Shit!" Jake pulled Lindsay to the center of the boat, as far from the gruesome tentacles as possible. "C'mon," he yelled at Brad, "let's get out of here."

Brad was already making his way to the wheel. He pushed the throttles forward, but the propellers seemed to churn slowly.

Below, countless Humboldt Squid threw themselves into the boat's twin props, sacrificing themselves until the boat's propellers, the only means of propulsion, were horribly jammed with squid carcasses.

"Go! Go!" Jake yelled.

"I'm trying," Brad yelled.

Mon, now roused from her drunken lethargy, stumbled forward to join her frantic comrades.

The boat lurched as the Giant Squid pulled down. The water around the boat now began to boil again with the return of hundreds of squid.

"Brad! Do something!" Mon screamed as the rocking boat made her fall to the deck.

"I'm trying!" Brad turned the engine on and off, pushing fruitlessly at the throttles.

The Giant squid now rocked the boat from side to side, water splashing into the boat.

"We're taking on water," Jake stumbled over and retrieved life preservers, handing one to each person.

"I'm not going in there!" Lindsay pointed at the water.

The boat was now filled with water up to everyone's knees.

"You may not have a choice," Brad said, as he fastened his own life preserver. He opened a compartment, removed a raft and pulled the cord to inflate it.

The Giant squid gave one last pull and the boat began its slow roll to the side, collecting more water, the four passengers screaming as they entered the domain of the squid.

SEVEN

"These developments are troubling," Professor Von Hell-Sink studied the pictures of the dead squid taken in the hotel room. "The size... I've never seen one so large. The animal has no bones; it needs the buoyancy of the water to support its mass. It should not be able to move across a room and attack a person. And yet... Look," he held out a piece of the squid. "It has an almost type of basic exoskeleton. I've never seen anything like it."

"Some kind of genetic anomaly?" Rick offered.

"Perhaps. And this," the professor held up a woman's shoe, a sexy high-heeled thong, with a stiletto heel that was half-metal.

Rick smiled, "Something you're not telling me, Professor?"

"I think perhaps the Professor is more of a peep-toe, sling back type," Helga observed dryly.

Professor Von Hell-Sink scrunched his eyebrows, unable to fathom their joke. "The Coast Guard brought me this, asking me to run tests on the DNA from the heel."

Rick took the shoe from the Professor and examined it, "And..."

"*Dosidicus gigas,* Humboldt squid."

"Where did this shoe come from?"

"The survivor of an apparent squid attack. The boat was sunk and three of the four people were lost." The Professor paused, "Probably eaten by squids. The young woman who owned this shoe found her way onto a life raft and fought the squids off with her shoe. When the Coast Guard picked her up she told a fascinating tale of a squid grabbing the boat and pulling it underwater."

"Do you believe her?"

"I have not interviewed the girl; she is in the hospital. But that is the story she told the Coast Guard." The professor nodded at the shoe, "There *is* evidence of squid. And the boat and the other three people are... Gone."

Rick handed the shoe back to the professor, "A fashion statement *and* a weapon. But I've never heard of a Humboldt pulling a boat underwater."

"No, you are correct. But an *Architeuthis,* perhaps one larger than we have ever encountered, might certainly be capable of such."

"Humboldts are bad enough," Rick said. "They're strong, agile, hunt in packs and their numbers seem endless. But an *Architeuthis... I can't imagine the hell involved in taking on one, or more, of those.*"

The professor nodded in agreement, "Yes, we know little about them, they are still a mystery to us. Squid are some of the oldest creatures; they have survived extinctions that wiped out other species." He shrugged, "Perhaps because they live in the deep waters of the oceans. But now," he pushed his glasses up on his nose. "After thousands of years of *man*, with his relentless fishing and technology, perhaps we have altered their food supply or environment. Squid and man will undoubtedly have more contact. We need more data, more samples."

Rick moved to the table and studied the map, "Here?" His finger pointed to a place on the map.

"Everything we know suggests it's the best place."

Rick nodded, "Alright, tonight… At Murphy's Point."

As he went to leave he found Helga blocking the door with her imposing, but seductive, Teutonic frame.

"Herr Steele, you will bring me something tonight?" Her blue eyes narrowed, focusing on his. She moved forward, placing a hand on his muscled chest, "Something large… And powerful, *Ja*?" Her pink tongue licked around her lips, "I hear you are a man who always delivers?"

Rick took her right hand in his, bringing it to his lips for a courtly kiss before he left. *"Bis Später, Liebchen."*

*****

The boat was buffeted by choppy waves, its passengers thrown about.

"Couldn't we have waited for a better night?" Jaime yelled over the crashing water as the bow of the boat pounded through the ocean swells.

Loida wiped spray from her face, her eyes bleary, "Can't afford to be scooped. This is *my* story. Those squids aren't going to come to us." She looked around the small open boat, her knuckles white as she held on. "I thought your cousin had a bigger boat."

"It's free," Jaime said, "you think the network is going to pay for a boat to go out and look for squids?" In the darkness he couldn't see Loida shrug her response.

"Ees not so bad," Miguel, Jaime's cousin yelled from the bridge. "Maybe she get smoother farther out." His laugh could be heard over the roar of the engine and the crash of the waves.

He was right, thirty minutes later, as they approached the drop-off of the continental shelf the frantic waves died down, but the swells continued to make Loida queasy.

"Here ees deep water," Miguel slowed the boat as he pulled the baseball cap down on his head.

Jaime started removing his camera from the waterproof bag while Loida tried to make herself presentable for a live report. Jaime looked around, there were a few lights on the horizon, a large tanker and a smaller boat or two, but essentially they were alone. "This the place? I mean, how would we know?"

Loida opened a lighted makeup mirror and touched up her lips. "Captain Hawk said to come out from the point, to the deep water, shine a light in the water and throw out a line. He said they'd find us." She did a three-sixty perusal of their location and her face didn't show confidence.

Miguel rigged the lights, "You look for *diablo rojo*, si? They come. You see."

Loida took down her ponytail and tried to fluff out her hair. "You've seen them, Miguel? Do you know why they are here?"

"I see many in Gulf of California. Squid everywhere, all seas," he stopped to scratch his chin, "but so many, here, now..." He shrugged and flipped the switch.

Loida blinked as the Halogen lights illuminated the surface of the sea. "Okay Jaime, let's do a take." She unzipped her windbreaker to show a bit of cleavage and ran her fingers through her hair. "This is Loida Enal live from a boat off Murphy's Point. We're here to investigate the invasion of Humboldt squid." She paused, "Let's see what we come up with and then we can add more."

She and Jaime relaxed as best they could in the pitching boat as Miguel prepared and dropped a line into the depths.

"Hey!" Miguel yelled, "You want to make video?" His muscular arms were hauling in the line, "I got squid."

Loida and Jaime were on their feet, Jaime trying to frame Loida in the lens with Miguel in the background. "We've just hooked one of the killer squid and are bringing it on board. The squids, it seems, are attracted to bright lights." She motioned Jaime over to get footage of Miguel bringing the squid in the boat.

With a grunt, Miguel hauled in the squid, the flailing animal landing with a 'plop' on the deck.

Loida gasped and backed away as Jaime continued to film the event.

Miguel smiled and spread his hands, "*Diablo rojo*, you want more?" He gestured to the ocean, "Many more, I think."

"No," Loida held up her hand, "no, not now, this is good." She leaned over to get a better look at the squid.

"Kneel down," Jaime urged, "get next to it."

Loida grimaced but knelt down, keeping her distance from the thrashing arms and tentacles. *This could get me a Sanchez award*, she thought. "This is the killer squid that has invaded the area and destroyed the fishing. How many more are there? Thousands? No one knows and no one knows what to do about them." She signaled Jaime to stop filming.

"When did they become *killer squids*?" Jaime asked. "I don't remember Captain Hawk or anyone else calling them killer squids."

"No one," Loida shot him a glare, "is going to watch

a news story about fluffy-kitten-squids. And they eat fish and stuff, kill it, so... Killer squids."

Miguel held the line, "You want more? I catch."

"Sure," Loida nodded, "more squids means a bigger story."

"Okay," Miguel smiled, "I catch." He dropped the line overboard.

*****

"What the hell are they doing?" Rick peered through the night-vision binoculars and watched the small boat with the three people haul in their third squid.

"Maybe they fish for squid, Boss." Choo, watched the light bobbing on the boat.

"Yea," Rick murmured, "but why and who are they?"

*****

The fourth squid landed on the deck and Loida struggled to get out of the way. "Eww," she kicked away a thrashing squid arm.

"Let me set up a shot with you and the squids," Jaime suggested.

As Loida knelt behind the pile of squids, a safe distance back, she felt the boat lurch and she tumbled across the deck to the other side, grabbing the gunwale with one hand to keep from falling overboard.

Jaime crashed into the side of the boat as well, turning to use his body to protect his video camera. "What the hell!" he exclaimed. He looked over to see Miguel crumpled next to him.

The boat was listing and Loida, Jaime and Miguel had all rolled to the starboard side.

"Miguel," Jaime shook his cousin and saw Miguel's eyes flutter open. "The boat, what's wrong?"

Loida tried to push herself up using her hand on the gunwale when she felt something wet on her hand. One of the lights used to attract the squid was broken and dangling, casting moveable shadows about the boat. When the light beam swung across her hand she saw a writhing tentacle and screamed. She pulled back her hand and tried to stand but slipped and fell on the wet and pitched deck.

The boat was jarred by several loud thumps and continued to list.

Miguel struggled to his feet and pulled a flashlight out of his pocket. When he ran the beam alongside the boat he saw the starboard side was full of squids, half out of the water, their tentacles clinging to the side of the boat, their accumulated mass threatening to tip the boat over. When he played the light over the water he saw more squids coming.

"They are sinking the boat!" Miguel yelled. He grabbed a piece of metal from the broken light mount and flailed away at the squid tentacles clinging to his boat. As soon as he beat away one creature, two more would join.

"Should we abandon ship?" Loida looked around for a life preserver.

"What?" Jaime pointed to the water around the boat, now teeming with squids. "In there?"

Water was now spilling over the side of the boat. "*Diablo rojo!*" Miguel screamed as he battled in vain against the squid onslaught.

Loida and Jaime searched for a higher refuge, but

found none on the small boat which was close to sinking.

The sound of a high-powered engine caught their attention as a boat cut through the night in their direction.

Loida and Jaime waved their hands toward the sound of the approaching boat, "Over here, help us, we're sinking!"

Rick expertly steered his boat, maintaining his high rate of speed and passing dangerously close to Miguel's sinking boat. Rick's powerful boat and the twin propellers cut a bloody swath through the squids who dispersed only momentarily before resuming their assault on the boat.

Rick turned again, slowing this time to come alongside the stricken craft.

Choo threw a rope to Miguel who used it to pull the two craft together long enough for Loida, Jaime and Miguel to jump into Rick's boat.

"Oh! Thank you," Loida rushed forward, but stopped short when she saw the stranger draw a wicked machete from its scabbard. Her eyes went wide to watch her tall and muscular savior swing around and hack off the tentacles off a squid trying to get in the boat.

"Boss," Choo yelled, "we go now!"

Rick pushed the throttles forward and the bow of the boat rose out of the water, cutting through the night, leaving a phosphorescent trail in its wake.

Left behind, the surviving Humboldt squid began to feed on the remains of their deceased comrades, darting back and forth, in and out, in a feeding frenzy. Finally, all became still and the squids descended once again into the deep.

EIGHT

Loida collapsed on a seat, with Jaime taking a place beside her. They rode in silence as their rescuer turned his craft for the shore. She looked up to see him silhouetted against the moonlight. He didn't look back at them, his attention fixed dead-ahead.

A short, muscular Asian man stopped in front of her. "You lucky lady," he gazed at her and Jaime and then went to join Rick.

Loida looked at the camera Jaime still held. "How much of that did you get?"

"Nothing after we slid on the deck. I'm lucky I still have the camera," he glanced back to see his cousin's boat slide under the water.

Loida rubbed her hands over her face and then through her hair. She stood, still uneasy on her legs, "I need to find out who Mr. Rugged Bad-Ass is and what he was doing out there."

Jaime flipped the switch on her camera and smiled when the red light illuminated. "You doing an interview?"

"No," Loida eyed the stranger, "he doesn't look like the talkative type. But keep it running, just the same."

Jaime winked as Loida walked forward.

She approached and watched as the Asian man looked her over and then moved to the back of the boat where he pulled out a flask and offered Miguel a drink.

"Thank you," Loida's voice, despite the recent

terrors, was now honeyed. "If you hadn't come when you—"

"Shouldn't have been out there," Rick's voice held no emotion.

"Excuse me?"

"You had no business being out there, in that boat, at night, messing with squids." Rick turned to look her up and down, his expression blank, and then turned his attention to the lights from the shore.

"Yes, I suppose so. Still, we're grateful. I'm Loida Enal, El Segundo Cable News." She changed her tone from conciliatory to flirtatious, "May I know the name of my gallant rescuer?"

Once again, he failed to look at her, "Steele, Rick Steele."

"And how did *you* come to be there?"

He greeted her inquiry with a stony silence.

She was not deterred. "What were those things?"

He cocked an eyebrow, "Specifically? *Dosidicus gigas, also known as the Humboldt Squid.* That what you were looking for tonight?"

She held her chin out defiantly, "Yes, we were."

For the first time his lips turned into a smile she found quite charming and he laughed, "Well then Ms. Loida Enal of El Segundo News, you found 'em. You sure as hell found 'em."

"We're doing a news story on why they are here and the impact they are having on the local fishing industry." She paused and bit her lower lip, "Do you have a statement to make on the issue?"

"Other than I saved your asses tonight?" He pretended to consider the question, "Nope."

Rick turned to nod at Choo as he joined them. "This is my crew," Rick said.

Loida extended her hand to Choo, "Thank you, your intervention was quite timely. I'm Loida Enal."

Choo took her hand and bowed, "Ah Choo."

"Bless you," Loida said.

Rick laughed, "His name, his *name* is Choo, *Ah Choo*."

"Oh… I… Uh, thank you," Loida said.

Choo flashed her a toothy smile as she backed away to resume her seat by Jaime, who was now sharing the flask with Miguel and offered it to Loida.

"Did you get any of that?" Loida sipped from the flask, the drink was strong, but she didn't know what it was.

"A bit," Jaime whispered, "hard to film secretly, at night on a moving boat."

"Rick Steele and his sidekick Ah Choo," she said. "We need to check them out when we get back to the office. I don't believe they were out here by accident and just happened by. They know something about this squid thing."

"Yea," Jaime took the flask from her and took a long pull, "I know something too."

Loida sat back and sighed, "What's that?"

Jaime looked back over the stern, to the flat, black ocean where cousin Miguel's boat now lay thousands of feet below on the sea floor. "I'm not goin' back out there. No way."

NINE

Rick dropped his passengers off at the harbor at Murphy's Point and then disappeared, his sleek and powerful boat *The Kraken* roaring off into the darkness.

Loida's attempts to engage him in further dialogue proved fruitless and he left her with a curt warning that the ocean was a dangerous place. She pulled out her damp notebook and scribbled down: Rick Steele, Ah Choo and *The Kraken*. *It's not much, but it's a start*, she thought. *Mr. Steele knows something; he's involved.*

*****

"Sorry professor, no samples." Rick threw his jacket over a chair. "Instead of a specimen collection it turned into a rescue mission."

"Rescue?" Von Hell-Sink scrunched his white bushy eyebrows. "Were there injuries? Who?"

"Some reporter," Rick gazed across the room, picturing the alluring Loida Enal, even under the circumstances of last night. "They were fishing for squids when they were attacked," he rubbed his stubbled chin. "I've never seen anything like it; a mass of Humboldts actually sank their boat. If Choo and I hadn't come along…" He let the thought trail off, imagining the three people struggling in the water as they were devoured piecemeal by a hoard of ravenous squids.

RICK STEELE: Squid Hunter

Rick detailed the encounter to the Professor, who listened with rapt attention.

Von Hell-Sink poured them each a shot of Schnapps.

"I've never seen anything like it," Rick tossed back the glass and held it out as the Professor filled it again. "So what now, Professor? You're the man with the plan; I'm just the executioner."

"This is not random," the Professor began to pace the room, his hands clasped behind him. "No, not coincidence. There is something behind this. A plan. An intelligence." A worried look crossed his face, "This… Or things like it, have happened before."

Rick narrowed his eyes, "And you know this… How? When? Where?"

"It was on Columbus' first voyage to the new world, his fourth ship was sunk. By an attack of squids."

"Fourth ship?" Rick chuckled, "There were only three, the *Niña, Pinta*—"

"That's what *they* want you to believe." The Professor opened a wooden box and unrolled a small leather scroll on the table. "The fourth ship, the *El Gato Negro* was sunk just days before the expedition made landfall at what we now know as Grand Turk." He paused to let it sink in as Rick leaned forward to look at the scroll.

"And that's what this says? I don't read Latin."

"It does," the Professor said. "It's an account of the attack written by a Brother Maynard, who accompanied Columbus on his first voyage. The actual records have been suppressed by the Vatican."

Rick fingered the edge of the scroll. "So… Where did you get *this*?"

"It was part of the Knights Templar treasure recovered from the Oak Island money pit."

"Wait," Rick stood upright, "I didn't think they'd ever found anything at Oak Island?"

The professor shrugged, "That's what they want you to believe."

"Again, who are *they*?"

"This," the professor tapped the scroll with his finger, his ring with the square and compass catching the light, "coupled with what we are experiencing now, tells me we have an old and powerful enemy." He stopped and paced. "There have been attacks before, throughout history, but these newest ones are much different. The squid seem more powerful, smarter."

Rick nodded, placed his glass on the table and picked up the beak from a Giant Squid. He ran his fingers over the hard, sharp edges. "Octopus are smart, they've shown problem-solving abilities, but squid…?"

"We have had more opportunity to study the octopus," the Professor observed, "squid, especially the larger species are more elusive. We don't know enough about them."

"We know they're fast and agile, they go almost anywhere they want and they can be deadly."

The Professor nodded, "But there's more, there has to be more."

Rick stood and grabbed his coat, "Tomorrow professor, right now I need a couple of drinks and some sack time."

The Professor, deep in thought, mumbled an unintelligible reply and waved his hand.

Rick started to exit the lab, only to find the door blocked by the sensual Helga.

Her blonde hair was released from the confines of the severe bun behind her head and now cascaded over the shoulders of her white lab coat. The coat itself was open revealing the stunning body normally hidden under long white lab attire. The top three buttons of her blouse were undone and Rick's eyes couldn't help but see her impressive cleavage.

The scents of Vanilla and Lavender wafted to him, a change from the normal sterile and disinfectant smells of the lab.

"*Herr* Steele, your expedition was successful, *Ja*?" She removed her black-framed eyeglasses slowly, batting her long dark lashes and sliding the glasses into the pocket of her lab coat.

"Sorry," his eyes twinkled, "I didn't get any specimens last night."

Helga narrowed her eyes and licked her lips. She moved even closer, placing her hand on his chest; she felt his warmth, his masculine power. "Really? I find that hard to believe. I am sure you have a... Most impressive specimen." Her hand trailed down his chest, lower, until she felt the outline of his throbbing crotch. "Permit me to examine *this*, *Bitte*?"

He pulled her close, her breasts crushing against his chest as he felt her hard, peaked nipples.

Her hand grabbed his hair at the back of the neck to hold him close as his lips descended on hers. Her other hand caressed him, and she felt him grow longer and harder in the confines of his jeans. Her lips parted as his tongue sought entry and she accepted his invasion eagerly.

She broke the kiss suddenly, pulling back, but maintaining her grip on his throbbing manhood. "I have a room," she whispered, releasing her grip, "here at the lab." She turned to walk down the hallway. Rick paused, sighed and followed her.

*****

"Hey boss," Choo waved from the bar.

Rick took a seat next to his comrade and accepted the beer Sam placed in front of him.

"Somethin' to eat?" Sam asked.

Rick looked at the hamburger on Choo's plate and nodded.

"Comin' right up."

"You tell professor?" Choo scooped up ketchup with a fry.

"Yea, he didn't like it," Rick turned to the stage to watch Lola and the band.

"Not good," Choo agreed, "I never see squid do that."

"What about our friends from last night?" Rick returned Lola's smile.

Choo took another drink of his beer and pulled out a notebook. "They check out. The woman is reporter." He turned on his phone and pulled up the station bio picture of Loida Enal.

Rick studied the picture. Drop-dead gorgeous in her bio pic, with long dark hair, luscious lips and smoldering eyes, she was even more of a knock-out than she'd been last night.

"The other man is cameraman. And his cousin, who owned the boat."

"Yea, too bad he had to lose his boat, but he shouldn't have been out there." Rick accepted his food from Sam. "Has there been anything on the news?"

"No, boss, that strange, huh? Boat attacked and sunk with a reporter there and no news story."

Rick washed down a mouthful of his hamburger with a swallow of beer. "Yea, reporters are all about the story, the scoop. Hmmm, that is odd. Keep an eye on the news."

"You got it, boss."

Rick held up his burger as Sam walked by, "This isn't Benny," he said, referring to Sam's short-order cook.

"Nah, Benny's wife had another kid; he's takin' a few days off. My sister-in-law's kid is cookin'. He was on some TV show chef contest, came in second, but still landed himself a job at a swanky New York restaurant. Said he was gonna be a Sue chef, don't know why they have to give him a girly name, but what the hell," Sam shrugged. "Hey kid," he yelled into the kitchen. "Come out here."

A dark-skinned young man with black curly hair stepped forward. He wore a white Chef's coat with 'Manilla' embroidered on his left chest. "Like it?" he nodded at Rick's burger.

"Excellent," Rick said. He extended his hand, "You are…"

"Salvatore," the young man said, "my Dad was from the old country, probably where I got my cooking skills, but most people call me—"

"Hey everybody," Sam yelled out to the club. His voice was full of pride as he said, "We got Sal Manilla in the kitchen tonight."

A silence fell over the club, followed by patrons spitting out food.

Sam held up his hands, "What…?"

*****

"You're not filing the story?" Jaime asked, incredulous.

"Not yet," Loida said. "There's some missing angles. When I go, I want to go big, so keep a lid on it."

"Okay," Jaime shrugged, "you're the star. Hey, what about my cousin? His boat?"

"Keep him quiet for now. Tell him the station will buy him a new boat."

Jaime's eyes widened, "Will they do that?"

Loida's lips split in a devious smile, "They might, if this story is as big as I think it is."

*****

Lola slinked from the stage and across the floor, stopping to give Choo a kiss on the cheek before she slid onto the stool next to Rick as he pushed away his empty plate. "That was my last set. Want to take me home?" She threw her long hair over one exposed shoulder of the skin-tight red sequined gown. One arm of the gown was long-sleeved and the bare-shouldered side had her arm covered in a long red glove.

Rick found the look seductive as he gazed into her green eyes. He ordered another beer and a Champagne cocktail for Lola. "Sure."

"We go out tomorrow night, boss?" Choo finished his beer.

Rick thought about his aborted mission that evening, ruined by his rescue of the sexy reporter. "Yea, we'll try again; see if we have better luck."

Choo stood, "I go back to boat. Get ready."

Lola turned on her stool and leaned over to hug Choo goodbye, the plucky sidekick inhaling the aroma of her perfume and smiling as he left the bar.

"The police were in here earlier this evening," Lola sipped her drink, "asking around if anyone heard anything about a shooting in a cheap hotel." She smiled and narrowed her eyes at Rick, "Looking for a well-armed, good-looking killer."

Rick shrugged, "Those squids aren't a protected species. I suppose they could charge me with discharging a firearm within the city limits."

She sat back, crossing her legs and allowing the thigh-high slit of her gown to fall over her leg exposing her stocking top and garter. "You could discharge your firearm within my limits."

Rick's eyes twinkled and his lips formed a devious grin as he signaled Sam for more drinks.

TEN

Loida pushed away from her desk and closed her eyes, giving herself a break from the last hour of grueling computer research. She opened her eyes and looked at her notepad, sighing at the relatively few notes she'd made. "So who the hell *are* you, Mr. Rick Steele?"

"Getting anywhere?" Jaime placed a cup of coffee on her desk.

She snorted, "It's almost like him or his sidekick don't exist. In this day and age, people leave computer footprints all over the place, there's always a trail. But these guys… Almost nothing." She nodded her thanks for the coffee and took a sip. She gazed across the studio offices, barely occupied at the late hour. "He comes out of nowhere to save our asses and is calm and cool when he whips out a machete to hack up one of those squids trying to get in his boat. He wasn't surprised by any of it, like a normal day at the office for him."

"Yea, well," Jaime pulled out a notebook, "the boat's registered to H-S Laboratories. The name, *The Kraken*, it's a mythical squid or octopus-like sea creature."

"Got that. What about the H-S labs?"

Jaime shrugged, "Not much. It's a private company and they don't really do any—business. I can't find them selling anything, or working with any government or university grants. They just seem to—be. There's no web site, no phone number; I only found them through the boat's registration. After that, it's a dead end. I did find something that said Steele came from Remulak, a small town in France." He watched as she began to type 'Remulak' into Google. "It's… Uh… That's not real." He stiffened his posture and raised his voice, "We are from Remulak, a small town in France." He watched Loida's face for recognition, but saw none.

She sighed, "I didn't do any better. No phone listing, no web activity. Maybe that name's a fake. Same for the inscrutable Ah Choo.

"Bless you," Jaime joked.

She rolled her eyes, "It's not funny the second time." She drummed a pencil on her desk, "This lack of information simply makes me believe that he *is* involved. Somehow."

"So…" Jaime sat on the edge of her desk. "What do we do? We don't even know where he lives."

"Any public record of where he keeps his boat?"

"I checked," Jaime said, "no record of a berth in any of the public docks. I do have an address for H-S Labs."

"It's thin," Loida rose from her chair and stretched, "but it's all we have right now." She glanced at her watch, "Pick me up at seven tomorrow morning and we'll check out H-S Labs."

*****

The morning sun sliced through the small crack in the blinds and Rick turned away, pulling the covers over his head. He caught the scent of Lola's perfume and buried his face in the pillow.

A noise from the kitchen made him look up and he

caught the aroma of coffee and frying bacon. He sat up on the bed and ran his fingers through his dark hair. Lola's gown from the night before hung from a hanger on the door and his clothes were strewn around the floor. Rick picked up his shorts and t-shirt and pulled them on, padding barefoot to the kitchen.

Lola was wearing a short robe that barely covered her well-rounded bottom. She glanced over her shoulder and blew him a kiss, "Sleep well?"

He poured himself a cup of coffee, "Eventually… After the sexual gymnastics."

Lola put a hand on her hip and assumed a sexy pose, cocking her head and letting her hair hang down loosely. "Not complaining are you?"

His strong arm wrapped around her waist and he brought her close for a smoldering kiss. "No. Definitely *not* complaining."

She turned back to the stove and started on the eggs. "So what happened last night? I get the impression things didn't go well for you and Choo."

He sat at the table and drank his coffee, watching her long, shapely legs that emerged from the short, silky robe and smiling at her perfectly painted red toenails. "We went out hunting and ended up conducting a rescue mission instead."

She placed the plates on the table and sat across from him. "Was anyone hurt?"

"No, but it was close. If we hadn't been there…" He watched as she ate, taking small bites, holding her fork just so, very ladylike, but *all woman.*

"I've got a session at the studio this afternoon,

recording a new song that Clifford wrote. Will I see you at the club tonight?"

"I don't know. Choo and I are going back out tonight."

She reached across and laid her hand on his, "You'll be careful."

*****

Jaime picked Loida up at seven a.m., bringing her coffee. "So we just look around today? Go to that H-S Laboratories and see what we find?"

"It's all we have, right now." She slid into the front seat of the van.

Forty-five minutes later they were parked by a water tank, watching a non-descript, windowless building through binoculars. "You're sure this is the place?" Loida adjusted the binoculars, bringing the building into focus.

"That's what my contact at the utilities billing office gave me," Jaime looked at the address he'd scribbled in his notebook.

"Doesn't look like what I pictured," Loida dropped the binoculars in her lap.

"What do you want to do? Go up and—" Jaime was cut off when Loida held up her hand.

They watched a black Mercedes sedan with tinted windows drive up and park by the building. A tall voluptuous blonde, dressed in a black suit and her hair tied in a severe bun got out of the car and entered the building as Jaime took photos of her.

"Get the license number of that Mercedes," Loida said, "let's see if we can track it down."

They waited in silence for another hour and a half when Jaime looked over his shoulder and poked Loida excitedly. "Look," he pointed frantically to the dock that was across the street from the parking lot of H-S Laboratories.

"*Madre de Dios*," Loida muttered. "It's *them*!"

Rick eased back on the throttles, bringing *The Kraken's* powerful twin engines to a muted roar as he expertly guided the boat into the slip across from the professor's lab.

"Video! Video," Loida poked Jaime.

Jaime filmed as Rick and Choo tied up their boat and walked across the parking lot and accessed the building with their own security cards.

"I wonder who else is in there," Loida mused, "and what, exactly, is going on? Can you have your contact at DMV run that Mercedes license? I'd like to know who the blonde is."

Ten minutes later Jaime shook his head, "The car is registered to, wait for it… To H-S Laboratories."

"Another dead-end," Loida let her head fall back against the headrest. "But at least we have Mr. Steele and his sidekick tied to the lab, *somehow*." She glanced over to the deserted boat. "I'm gonna go have a look."

Jaime started to get out of the van, but was stopped by Loida. "Stay here," she took her cellphone from her purse. "Call me if they come out."

Jaime knew better than to argue with ace reporter Loida Enal, so he took his seat and resumed his surveillance of the building.

Loida walked to the boat in a calm manner, yet totally out of place with her skirted suit and stiletto heels on a waterfront. She slipped and fell into Rick's boat as she tried climb down the wooden adder from the dock to the boat. Loida dusted herself off, straightened her skirt and began exploring *The Kraken.*

She hadn't really paid much attention to the boat on the night of her rescue, but now she went forward, into the small, but modern cabin. It seemed well equipped with any number of hi-tech communication and navigation equipment, and many things she couldn't identify. She took pictures with her phone, while looking for any kind of log book or written documentation, which she did not find.

Loida tried to turn on the laptop that was part of the electronics suite, but it was password protected. Some of the cabinets and drawers were locked and those that weren't contained only food, clothes or the standard boating supplies and equipment.

"And the mystery continues," she huffed to no one in particular.

She went back out on deck, glancing over at the H-S Labs building and then down the street to the van with Jaime. All was quiet.

Loida's eyes settled on something that definitely had not been on the boat during their rescue. She walked to the stern and lifted the tarp that covered *something.* It took a moment for her to identify the giant harpoon gun. Her eyebrows furrowed in question. *They're not out to kill whales, so what is this for?* She rummaged on deck, finding nothing out of the ordinary, except for more locked compartments.

*****

Professor Von Hell-Sink, Helga, Rick and Choo all stood studying a map of the coastline.

"Here, here, here *und* here," the Professor pointed to red dots on the map.

Rick's finger traced a line made by the dots, "Here's where I rescued the reporter, where the kids in the boat were killed, and two other unreported incidents."

"Yes, yes," the professor shook his head vigorously, "they seem to be following the current that runs up the coast. If you go out tonight and troll these areas, maybe you will find something."

"Sounds like a plan," Rick agreed. "Choo and I will prep the boat today and go out this evening. Do you have that special equipment we talked about?"

ELEVEN

Loida's phone rang as she continued to search Rick's boat. It was Jaime. "Loida, there's some activity at the building. A big roll-up door opened and a van drove out. Looks like Steele and Choo are loading up some kind of equipment. I can't tell what it is. Maybe you should get out of there."

"Okay, Jaime, I'm on my way." She hurriedly tried to put everything in place to leave no trace of her search. She peered up over the edge of the dock, and when she saw it was deserted she made her way back to the van.

Back at the van she took the bottle of water Jaime offered. "So what's been happening," she asked between sips.

He handed her the binoculars, "Nothing after you went to the boat. It was quiet for quite a while, then that door opened up, the van pulled out and Steele and his sidekick started loading things into it."

She watched as Steele talked to the tall blonde in the white lab coat. "What things?"

"Couldn't tell. Boxes, things that looked like footlockers."

Loida focused the binoculars to watch the blonde give Steele a coy smile and then step inside as the door closed. She watched as Choo got into the driver's seat, Steele jumped in the passenger side and they drove the equipment-laden van to the dock, parking it as close to their boat as possible. "What are you up to, Mr. Steele?"

Steele and Choo used a two-wheel dolly to move their cargo to the boat, taking three such trips to transfer everything. Loida watched intently as they spent another forty-five minutes securing their gear.

Finally, Rick got in the van and drove it back into the building, the door opening as he approached and closing as the van entered the facility.

Loida turned her gaze back to Choo, who remained, working on the boat.

Jaime slouched in his seat and looked at his watch. "Now what?"

"We wait," Loida said, "no one ever said being a reported was all glamour. We wait and watch. They're up to something."

*****

They waited. Luckily, Jaime brought water and snacks, because Steele stayed in the H-S Laboratories building all day while Choo was visible now and again as he continued to work on *whatever* on the boat.

"Somethin's up," Loida nudged Jaime. She watched Choo through the binoculars as he answered his phone and then began to climb off the boat and on to the dock. "He's going back to the building."

Jaime watched Choo walk across the street, "Yea, so…"

"I'm going back to the boat," Loida said.

"I don't think that's such a good idea," Jaime's voice held concern. "It's going to be dark soon; we don't know what they have planned. You got lucky the last time." He put his hand on hers. "Let's wait and watch."

"That time has passed." She gave his hand a motherly pat and then removed it from hers. "A good reporter waits and watches," she opened the van door, "but they also investigate." She nodded at the building. "Call me if they come out."

Jaime watched her walk away toward the boat. The setting sun framed her voluptuous figure; she looked like a Goddess walking into the sun, with the ocean in the distance. He picked up his camera to film the scene, *Might be good for a trailer.*

*****

The professor finished his pre-mission briefing for Rick and Choo. "Be careful, Rick," the professor warned. "If there is an *Architeuthis,* or worse, more than one, it could be very dangerous. We know little about them, but if they have some of the intelligence and problem solving abilities of the octopus, and the communicative pack-hunting of the Humboldts, that could prove formidable."

Rick clasped a large hand on the professor's shoulder. "That's why Choo and I are prepared. Unlike their previous victims, we know they're out there, and we're ready for them."

"Helga and I will be monitoring the radio and any live video feeds you can send." The professor shook Rick and Choo's hands, "Good luck."

*****

Loida found that Choo had installed lights and several video cameras on The Kraken. The mysterious footlockers were secured to the deck, but were also locked, denying her access to their precious and probably newsworthy contents.

Her phone vibrated in her hand, she'd silenced the ringer. It was Jaime, "Crap! They're halfway to the boat!"

"What?" she half-yelled, half-whispered.

"I guess I wasn't paying attention," Jaime said, "and they're walking over, not driving, so I missed 'em. Get out, now."

She heard the heavy male footfalls on the wooden dock. "Too late," she whispered.

Jaime heard the phone go dead.

TWELVE

Loida's petite, but curvy, frame barely fit into the storage space beneath the cushioned seating in the boat's small cabin. Wherever they were going, the water was choppy that night, but as cramped as she was in her hiding place, she wasn't thrown about much.

She'd scarcely had time to hide and was now thinking twice about her decision to seek refuge. *Maybe I should have stayed on the boat, confronted them and tried to get my story.* Yet she knew that wouldn't have gotten her anywhere. The stoic and resolute Mr. Rick Steele would have sent her packing and sailed off to… Wherever. *No, the story is out there, somewhere. And I'm going to get it.*

She glanced at her phone and then remembered she'd turned it off, trying to save what battery life she had left. If there *was* a story, her phone would be the only way to document it with pictures and video.

The roar of the engines abated to a dull throb and the relentless chop and banging against the waves stopped. Loida felt the swell of the ocean and heard footsteps on the deck above.

On deck, Choo and Rick went about their business in an efficient and professional manner. Choo rigged the outboard floodlights and video cameras. Rick pulled the tarp from the harpoon gun and unlocked one of the footlockers, removing one of the deadly harpoons and loading the gun. He placed other barbed harpoons in a rack for quick access to reload.

Choo spoke into his headpiece as he turned on the video cameras. "You see okay, Professor?"

"Yes, Choo, the reception is quite good. Turn off the lights and try the night-vision cameras."

Choo turned off the lights and the Professor watched his screen image change to a ghostly green. He nodded with approval, whatever the conditions that night; they should be able to obtain much-needed video evidence.

"Professor," Rick also wore a headset, "I think we're ready."

"Excellent, excellent," the professor pulled his chair closer to the banks of monitors in his laboratory.

Rick nodded at Choo, "Okay, let's go fishing."

Choo smiled a full, toothy smile, switched the floodlights back on and dropped baited lines over the side.

Loida raised the lid of her hidey-hole, squinting through the crack to see the world outside brightly illuminated. The lights on deck turned the dark night into day.

She eased out of her confined space, taking a moment to stretch out her sore and cramped muscles. She'd kicked off her shoes when she crawled into her hiding place, and now she padded barefoot and silent to the cabin door. She heard Rick and Choo talking about lights and cameras. Loida looked at her cellphone and decided she didn't have any good picture or video opportunities yet, so she kept it off. *There's nothing going on down here, it's all going to happen up there*. She took a deep breath, opened the cabin door and climbed up on deck.

The boat looked different than when she had boarded earlier. Tanks and hoses took up space by the stern. Different weapons were placed in racks, ready-at-hand. Bright searchlights now glowed on the surface of the water. Then there was Rick, the man loomed large against the glare of the lights and gave Loida a lump in her throat. His back was to her and even though he wore a tactical vest, she saw his broad shoulders tapering down to a narrow waist. A short-barreled shotgun was in a scabbard on his back and the machete she'd seen him wield with deadly skill the night he rescued her was on his left hip. A shoulder holster held his Glock handgun. He looked dangerous, *He always looks dangerous*, she thought. She was unaware of her lips curving into a devious smile. *Dangerous. And all man.*

Choo was the first to see her; he shook his head and grinned, "Hey, Boss, we got passenger."

She flashed Choo a smile, noting he was also well-armed.

Rick turned and narrowed his eyes as Loida stood defiantly before him. "There are international conventions to deal with stowaways. There have even been incidents where the captain has put the stowaway overboard in anything that floats, giving them food and water and setting them adrift."

"I believe *you* to be more civilized," Loida said.

"I *could* lock you up and turn you over to the authorities for breaking and entering, and trespassing when we return." Rick turned his gaze to watch the surface of the water and then back to Loida. "What are you doing here, on board my boat?"

"I'm a reporter and I'm getting the story on those squids. Why are they here? What do they want?" She stepped closer to Rick, "And what is *your* role in all of this?"

"It's their world," Rick pointed to the ocean, "and as long as they stay there it's not my problem. When they encroach on man, they need to be stopped."

"Hey, boss," Choo yelled, "they coming."

Loida's frustration over Rick failing to answer her questions was overtaken quickly by the tightening of her stomach. She'd barely escaped death the last time she was confronted with the squid peril.

"Get in the cabin," Rick said, "stay inside. I can't do my job and worry about you."

"Do your job, Mr. Steele," she turned on her phone and selected the video option.

Choo hauled up one of the baited lines, his muscular arms pulling the line hand-over-hand, "Women, huh, boss?" He pulled the squid over the side, the creature landing on deck, its arms flailing.

Loida balanced herself on the rolling deck, getting all the action on video on her phone. "This is Loida Enal reporting from *The Kraken*." She saw Rick shoot her a disapproving glare. "Okay, okay, I'll edit that out."

Rick opened a hatch on deck and Choo used his foot to push the squid into the holding tank below.

Choo peered into the tank, "Maybe only get three or four if they all big."

"That'll be enough, keep fishing," Rick scanned the surface of the water, "and keep watching for the big one."

Loida leaned over to snap a picture of the squid in the tank before Rick kicked the hatch shut.

The water around the boat churned as Humboldt squid surfaced in the light and then dived down again. Loida moved cautiously to the side to take video of the squid frenzy. She jumped back and yelled when a squid attacked the side of the boat, slapping at it with its tentacles.

"I told you," Rick watched the squids, never taking his eyes off them; "you'll be safer in the cabin."

She took a video of the roiling water and the masses of squids. "Are you going to kill them?" she asked.

"Not as long as they stay in their own world, the ocean." Rick turned to glare at Loida, "I hunt them when they encroach or endanger us." He watched her eyes go wide and followed her gaze back to the side of the boat, where groups of tentacles were now clinging over the side.

"They're trying to sink us," she screamed, "like the other night." Loida backed away toward the cabin.

Rick's right hand pulled the machete from its scabbard as he brought it down severing three tentacles and sending the squid back into the water.

Frightened, but driven by *the story*, Loida crept forward, taking video of the wounded squid flailing in the water. "Oh my God!" She pointed to the water. "They're eating it! The other squids are eating one of their own." She watched as other Humboldts rushed in, tearing away hunks of flesh from the wounded squid with their sharp and powerful beaks.

"They'll do that. The Humboldts are opportunistic feeders, they'll eat almost whatever they can find. Including their own." He smiled, "But it distracts them from us for the moment."

"Hey, Boss," Choo yelled, "big one here."

Rick went over to help Choo haul in the Humboldt, larger than the last one. They dropped it in the holding tank.

"One more should do it," Rick said, "then let's get out of here, take the Professor his samples." He scanned the water, ever watchful.

The boat lurched suddenly, thrust up from the bottom with a powerful blow that almost sent Choo over the side. Loida tumbled to the deck and backed away toward the cabin door.

Rick's hand went for his machete, "Everybody stay calm."

"Squid on!" Rick yelled as enormous feeding tentacles wrapped around each side of the boat. His machete slashed out again, a piece of squid feeding tentacle falling to the deck as the tentacle oozed squid-essence and slipped back over the side.

Opposite Rick, the stalwart Choo did the same, attacking a tentacle between shouts of Oriental cursing that were indecipherable to Loida. Her shaking hands gripped the phone at her side. Her frightened eyes took in the scene; the sea around them was alive with squid; she felt and heard them as they slammed against the boat. "W-We should leave," she stammered.

"Ya think?" Rick's narrowed eyes scanned the ocean.

She screamed as the body of the Giant Squid rose slowly from the water at the stern of the boat.

"Now, Boss?" Ah Choo yelled.

"Now!" Rick slipped in behind the harpoon gun as Ah Choo flicked the stand-by generator to 'on'.

With the squid filling his sights at nearly point-blank range, Rick fired the harpoon gun. The wicked barbed projectile exploded from the gun, trailing a length of high-tensile cable. Sparks flew when it hit the squid, as ten-thousand volts pulsed into the giant beast.

It flailed in the water, a tentacle shooting out and barely missing Ah Choo.

Loida stood, speechless, the phone clutched in her hand at her side. She was witnessing the battle of a lifetime. And filming the deck.

"It's not enough current, Boss!" Ah Choo yelled.

The Professor's briefing about the new equipment ran through Rick's mind. "Most generators only go to 'ten'," the Professor had said. "This one has been modified, so if you need that extra, to go over the edge, you can turn it up."

"Turn it up to eleven," Rick ordered.

Sparks flew and steam rose from the ocean around the squid as it slipped into the water.

"Get a line around it, quick," Rick ordered.

Loida caught her breath and brought a shaky hand up to look at her phone. It was off. She turned it on, but the screen remained black. *Battery's dead. Great.* She wiped wet strands of hair from her face as she watched Rick and Ah Choo tie a line around the Giant Squid. "Is… Is it dead?"

Rick shrugged, "Probably. Could be stunned. Paralyzed. Who knows?"

"What are you going to do with it?"

"Take it to Professor," Ah Choo gave a toothy grin.

"We come out for small ones, but bring him back big one."

She moved warily to the side of the boat. Dead squid floated on the water, bobbing up and down as other squid came up to tear at them. "Will there be more? Are they coming back?"

"Don't know," Rick said, "and in any case, we won't be here." He climbed behind the ship's wheel and pushed the throttles forward. He turned to look back at Ah Choo, "Keep a watch back there."

Ah Choo waved a reassuring hand as his eyes roamed the surface and the Giant Squid trailing behind them.

*****

Jaime was jarred awake from the guttural sound of the boat's engines as it idled up to the dock. The sun was only beginning to light up the sky, but he clearly saw the shapely form of Loida stalk from the pier toward the van.

She slammed the door behind her and slumped into the seat.

Jaime rummaged in the cooler to find and hand her a bottle of water.

Loida nodded her thanks, took a long drink and closed her eyes.

"So, wanna tell me what happened?" Jaime took in her disheveled appearance and the dark circles under her eyes; obviously it had been a long night. "You were gone all night; I didn't know what to do so—"

She held up her hand to silence him and took a deep breath. "You did the right thing, thanks for being here," she laid her hand on his.

"Did you get the story?"

"Yea," she forced out a half huff-chuckle, "one *hell* of a story. But what I can prove…" She threw him her phone, "Battery's dead, but I might have gotten enough."

Jaime started charging her phone, "So what did you see?"

She stared out the van windows, watching as Rick and Ah Choo finished securing the boat. "Remember when we were out on that boat—and the squids attacked?"

Jaime nodded.

"It was like that. Only worse. More squids. Bigger squids, including the biggest I've ever seen. Our Mr. Rick called it a Giant Squid, an archa-something. *And*, they brought it back."

"Great!" Jaime opened the videos on Loida's phone. "Nothing here but them pulling up some squids like those other fishermen, picture of a squid in a holding tank. Nothing more."

Loida closed her eyes and sighed.

"Where's the Giant Squid and—"

"I didn't get it! Okay? There was all this action and then… Then… The battery died. Crap!"

"This Giant Squid they brought back, where is it?"

She blew out a breath, "They locked me in that little room they call a toilet on the boat. For an hour. I don't know where they went, it was still dark out when they finally let me out and by then the squid was gone."

"They stashed it somewhere," he turned off the phone. "So we have nothing, back to square one."

"Maybe not," Jaime said. "I got a call from my cousin, Ernesto, while you were out on your adventure. He said he was working as a cook down at some secret lab or something south of here, on the coast. We should check it out."

She closed her eyes, letting her head drop to her chest, "Tomorrow, okay? Take me home, I need a shower and some sleep."

*****

Professor Von Hell-Sink studied the massive squid in the holding tank, "And you say the others disappeared when you killed the *Architeuthis*?"

"Yea," Rick answered, "they stopped attacking the boat, mostly disappeared from the surface except for a few stragglers feeding on their dead comrades."

The professor rubbed his chin, "Most interesting. What we know of *Architeuthis* is that it seems to be a solitary predator, and will feed on other squid. Yet from what you are saying," he pulled down his glasses to look at the squid more closely, "there seemed to be some symbiotic relationship between the various squid species when they attacked your boat. Yes-s-s... Most interesting."

Rick shrugged, "Sorry it's dead. I mean, it's not like you're gonna be able to examine a live one."

"True," the Professor chuckled, "a live *Architeuthis* would have been a real find. But, my dear boy, I'm glad the squid is dead. And not you." He looked up to see Helga pushing in a cart, "We will do a necropsy, see if we find anything interesting."

THIRTEEN

Her admin poked her head around the open door. "Madame Secretary, Admiral Seez is on the secure line."

"Thank you, Paula," Anita Mann picked up the secure line as Paula closed the door.

She sat back in her executive chair and crossed her legs, "I hope you have good news for me, Admiral."

"Yes, Ma'am. We've located the specimen and are preparing to recapture it. My crews are getting the retrieval ship ready."

"I'm flying out to Argus Field now," Secretary Mann said. "Have someone meet me and my aide. You and I are going to be on that ship and make sure this gets done. Right."

"Madame Secretary, my crew is more than capable. I assure you—"

"Then there shouldn't be any problems. Should there?" Her tone was icy. "We'll just be along for the ride, to watch it all happen as you say. Yes?"

"Of course, Madame Secretary; I'll have transport at the airfield to take you directly to the ship when you land." He ended the call and paced his office. *This isn't getting any better.*

Anita Mann walked into the outer office area. "Paula, call Andrews, get my plane ready for a flight to Argus Field. Call my aide, Steven and tell him to meet me at Andrews."

*****

"It's a little rough out today," Admiral Seez suppressed a smile as Secretary Mann's aide, Steven's eyes glazed with each lurch of the ship. "We can turn back, let you two off."

Secretary Mann gripped a handhold, her knuckles turning white. "No! I want to make sure this gets done. Right. We're here to the end."

"I have a lock," a crewman said. "It's come up now. Receiving signal and data returns."

The ship's Captain bent over the crewman's shoulder, looking at the display. "Make course three-one-zero."

"Aye, Sir, course three-one-zero," the Helmsman repeated.

"It's leading us out to deeper water, off the continental shelf," Admiral Seez looked at both the compass heading and depth gauge.

"Where is Dr. Theerie?" Secretary Mann asked as the ship's bow broke another wave, sending water crashing over the ship.

"He stayed behind to run more data evals and prepare for the creature's return." He looked at the screen display; they were closing on their target. "Don't worry, we have sufficient men and equipment for one squid."

"Signal increasing, Sir, getting more data," the crewman said. More metadata about the target filled the screen. "Uh... Sir?" The crewman's voice took on a worried tone. "This signal..." He watched '**20**' appear on the display screen. "It's number t—"

Admiral Seez clamped his hand on the crewman's shoulder in what appeared to be a paternal gesture, but was in fact a vise-like grip. "That's right son, it's a number to follow."

The crewman nodded, "Yes, Sir. I... Understand."

*****

Thirty minutes ahead of them, the most intelligent, most aggressive and powerful squid the world had ever known hung silently in the depths. Suddenly, the water around the squid filled with a sea of flashing red and white. Thousands of Humboldt squid darted through the water, changing color. Waiting.

*****

"Target dead ahead, Sir. It's holding position. Depth, fifteen-hundred feet."

"Slow to one-third," the Captain ordered. "Crews to retrieval stations."

"Is it too deep?" Secretary Mann asked.

The Admiral nodded. "Yes, but we'll lure it up with baited lines to where our equipment can be used."

The sea had calmed, but the ship still rolled in the swells and both Secretary Mann and her aide struggled to keep their footing.

"Bait lines deployed," came the crackle of one of the deck hands over the intercom.

Admiral Seez pointed outside, "We have two lines on each side, port and starboard. Each line has a variety of attractors: lights, live bait and scent baits."

RICK STEELE: Squid Hunter

In the depths below, hundreds of squid gathered by each bait line. On some unknown, silent cue, they attached themselves to the lines.

Suddenly, the squids on the port side lines dove into the depths with all their strength, pulling as hard as they could. When they reached their limits, they relaxed their efforts as the squids on the starboard side made their own power dive to the black depths.

As the squids set the ship to rolling left and right, another group of squids attacked the ship's propellers in a suicide attempt to jam them and deprive the ship of power.

"Target acquired!" a crewman yelled as the first lines were attacked and the ship lurched to the side.

The ship's Captain and the Admiral shared a congratulatory handshake when the first lines were hit. Their joy was short-lived, however, when the ship lurched to the other side and began its rolling motion.

The Captain realized the imminent peril to his ship, "We're in danger of capsizing; cut the bait lines! All ahead full!"

"Belay that," the Admiral countermanded.

"Captain!" the Helmsman yelled, "I canna' give ya' more power. The ship can't take it."

"Bring up the target," Admiral Seez ordered. The rate of the ship's roll increased. Damage control sirens began to sound.

A deckhand slipped and fell into the sea. Even as his crewmates threw him a life preserver and a line they watched in horror as he was attacked and pulled, screaming, under the water by hordes of squids.

"Cut the lines," the Captain ordered.

As crewmen armed with bolt cutters moved to sever the thin steel cable, a pair of huge tentacles rose from the churning sea and swept across the deck, taking all exposed crew members to their doom.

The Admiral tossed life jackets to Secretary Mann and her aide. "If you can find something that floats, grab hold." He turned to the crew, "Issue a Mayday. Ship in distress; we're going down."

The distress call was cut short as water filled the bridge. The ocean was turned into a maelstrom of carnage. Squids attacked the screaming crew, pulling them under.

When the cries of human-kind ceased to fill the air the squids began to rip apart each piece of flotsam. The wind and currents carried the debris away. It was as if the ship, and its crew, had never existed.

EPILOGUE

The two men in black suits walked from the elevator, down the hall and waited for admittance to the office. When the green light over the door illuminated they went in.

Another man, in a black suit, sat behind a desk. His face was expressionless, "The site is sanitized?"

"It is," answered one of the men. "Herr Geld purchased the land and donated it to the state as a youth camp and the dock for a sea adventure program. The buildings have been vacated, stripped of all equipment."

The man behind the desk nodded. "The ship with Admiral Seez and Secretary Mann?"

The second standing man spoke, "Extensive surface searches have revealed nothing. Perhaps when they start probing the sea floor, but for all intents and purposes it's gone."

"And the reporter?"

The first man spoke, "She showed up, a tip from someone probably. Some of our team were there. They showed her and her cameraman around, let them look at everything, told them about the new camp for kids and they went away."

The second man spoke, "The next night she was doing a feature on some teen star undergoing rehab. Do you want us to maintain surveillance?"

"No," the man behind the desk said. "We tapped her

phone, we're reading her e-mails." He handed the men before him a file. "This is your next assignment."

*****

"Captain!" The four-star General yelled through the cigar clenched in his teeth. He pointed angrily to the breakfast tray on the credenza. "You tell Sergeant Sholts I do *not* eat breakfast cereal. Tomorrow it had better be bacon and eggs or you and Sholts will wake up the next morning deployed to some third-world sand pit!"

"Sir! Yes, Sir." The Captain removed the offensive tray and backed from the room.

General Mills turned to his guests. "Sorry for that, gentlemen."

"I quite understand," Dr. Theerie said. "It's just as easy to get these things right as it is wrong."

The General removed his cigar and punctuated the air as he exclaimed, "Ex-actly." He looked again at the file on the table and leaned back as he gazed at the men sitting around the conference table. "Sounds like some kind of comic book, science-fiction stuff." He stared at his chief science and technology officer, "Colonel?"

Colonel Kleenk stood and walked to a large digital display as charts and graphs began to illuminate. "The science *is* ambitious, General, but Dr. Theerie and Herr Geld," he nodded to the two men at the table, "have made significant progress and established much of the biological and technological groundwork."

General Mills used his short, stubby finger to scratch his buzz-cut head. "I don't know. Dr.," he looked up. "I didn't get your first name."

Dr. Theerie smiled, "It's one of those Eastern European ones, with too many consonants. Because I'm tall and thin my colleagues simply call me, 'String'."

General Mills nodded, "Okay, so, Dr. String... Theerie, you want to create a bunch of," he thumbed through the pages in the file, "Super High-Intensity Terror Chupacabras." He narrowed his eyes at Dr. Theerie, "I thought these Chupacabra things were legends. Myths."

"They most assuredly are not," Dr. Theerie said with finality. "Think of the advantages of having thousands of such creatures at your disposal and control. Imagine their use in modern urban warfare. They could take streets, buildings, rooms, saving the lives of your soldiers." He raised his hands, "The enemy are eliminated, your soldiers move in to merely occupy and hold the new territory."

General Mills leaned forward, "Keep talking."

Two Months Later

Rick guided his boat in and shut everything down as Choo made the mooring lines fast. Both men then went to the lab to report their latest findings to the professor.

Rick's finger traced a line over the map, marking their latest cruise. "Nothing," Rick said. "No unusual activity."

The professor nodded, "Yes, this correlates to the recent Coast Guard and fishing reports. The recent squid menace seems to have abated. The locals say the fishing is improving." He stroked his beard.

"So, professor?" Rick asked. "You learn anything from dissecting the Giant Squid we hauled in?"

"Its brain was larger, much larger than what we typically encounter. We know that Octopus are intelligent, good at problem solving. There is no reason to think this might not be true for the Squid as well." He motioned Rick over to a tray. "This specimen has been modified." He pointed to a blackened circuit board. "Your electrical shock to the squid probably saved your lives, but it destroyed this piece of electronics that was embedded in the squid's brain. Perhaps…" He paused and looked to the remains of the Giant Squid in the preservative tank, "Perhaps nature occasionally provides us with a super-Squid, one of exceptional intelligence and ambition. That would account for the episodes, however brief, throughout history. But someone has genetically modified this specimen."

Rick picked up the circuit board, noting the number seventeen. "Seventeen? Could there be more? He pondered the consequences, "And if it became the norm? Rather than the exception?"

The professor chuckled, "Then mankind may become a land-locked species." He turned to Rick, "It seems, for now, the crisis is averted."

"I'll be around, Professor, if you need me," Rick said.

"I do need you," the Professor said. "To go to the Southwest, to investigate several Chupacabra sightings around Roswell, New Mexico."

Rick paused and eyed the Professor, "You wouldn't happen to know anything…"

The Professor raised his eyebrows and removed a

scroll from a cabinet. "It seems that when Coronado left the Seven Cities of Cibola…"

*****

Deep within the Indian Ocean, Archetuthis specimen number 20, now double in size, floated in the depths as more squids gathered around it.

The END?

Rick Steele returns in:

RICK STEELE
versus
The Mongolian Death Python

Enjoy this excerpt from:
RICK STEELE versus The Mongolian Death Python:

Prologue:
The Chupacabra Affair

It had been a bloody affair. Rick Steele and his stalwart sidekick Ah Choo still didn't even know if it was over. They sat in the Albuquerque airport, nursing beers, trying to make sense of it all.

A curvy and well-endowed, bleach-blonde waitress came by for the second time in two minutes to check on her customers. She flashed her best smile at the rugged man with the black hair and piercing eyes. "You boys need another round?"

Rick smiled back, "We're good, thanks."

She leaned over to wipe their table, her breasts moving more than the bar rag. "Well, you need anything else," one red fingernail pointed to the nametag riding above her left breast, "I'm Tammy."

Rick nodded, "Thank you… Tammy."

She turned and walked away, Choo's eyes glued to her swaying hips.

"Hey, boss, maybe—"

Rick's stare cut Choo off. "Not now. And not her." Still, he did turn and give an approving nod as Tammy bent over to fill a napkin holder, her tight skirt stretching over an impressive backside.

He shook his head, trying to focus on what they'd been through; none of it made sense.

With the threat of the Giant Squid menace temporarily abated, Doktor Von Hell-Sink had sent them to investigate the reports of Chupacabra infestation around Roswell, New Mexico. They'd tracked the creatures to an isolated military testing ground, surrounded by a tall electric fence topped with razor wire. Steele and Choo set out camera traps and then settled in with night vision goggles to wait.

They saw the first signs at sundown, a large truck in military camo stopping by the fence as a gate in the fence slid open by remote control. The truck backed up to the opening, a hatch opened, and a dozen wiry, snarling mammals were discharged onto the high desert floor. They milled about, sniffing the air. Suddenly a high-pitched beeping sounded in the night. The animals looked up, their pointed ears flattening at the sound as they bounded off into the night.

Choo looked at Rick and whispered, "Like some kinda dog whistle? Maybe somebody controlling them?"

Rick nodded, "Be my guess." He pulled down the night-vision goggles and watched the frenzied green dots disappear over a distant ridge. "Seen all we can here. Get the camera traps and let's follow these things." Rick slipped down the dirt slope to start the Hummer as Choo gathered up the camera traps.

As he was about to start the Hummer he paused and cocked his ear. A low whirring sound came across the desert and then dust kicked up as a black helicopter flew overhead, travelling in the direction of the Chupacabra pack.

Choo jumped in the vehicle, stowing the cameras in the back. He nodded to the helicopter that disappeared into the night. "I dunno, boss, military, off-limits area, low observable helicopter flying with no lights, following a pack of those animals." He shook his head, "Not good."

Rick put the vehicle in gear and pulled down his night vision goggles. "I agree; these aren't simply a pack of rogue animals. It's obviously some kind of project, but by who—and why?"

They tracked the animals most of the night, watching as they pack-hunted and killed rabbits and even two coyote. The black helicopter made appearances, seeming to track the animals and then disappearing into the night. Two hours before dawn the pack stopped and again answered the call of the high-pitched sound. Rick and Choo watched as six of the animals scurried off further into the desert while the rest ran off in the direction they'd come, back to the anonymous top-secret military installation.

Choo scrunched his brows, "They separate?"

"Yea." Rick was grim. "That doesn't feel right. We'll follow those," he pointed to the six trotting off into the distance.

*****

The Major walked the length of the holding pens, watching the snarling beasts. "You say six ran off?"

"Sir," the Sergeant snapped to attention. "Yes, Sir, they didn't answer the signal."

"They all have locator tags?"

"Yes, Sir, we're geo-tracking them."

The Major scowled; he didn't like problems. "And our chopper pilots reported a vehicle out there last night?"

"A civilian Hummer, Sir, two occupants. They just watched. Probably cryptozoologist nuts or someone trying to sell a documentary to TV."

The Major frowned; he was not happy. "Maybe. Maybe not. Contact Dr. Theerie, find out why those six ran off." He glared at the Chupacabras, "If we can't control these things I'm shutting the project down." He considered the situation. "Wire this place with the charges; if we can't contain this then all I want if anyone comes around here is a big hole in the desert. Do it, Sergeant."

"Sir, yes, Sir."

*****

Sister Mary Margaret Murphy said a prayer under her breath. She turned and walked back to the bus. "Girls!" She watched as the busload of fresh-faced young cheerleaders dressed in short, red plaid skirts and low-cut, tight white sweaters, all from St. Helens School for Girls, looked her way. "Someone is coming to fix the tire thing, so we'll have to wait."

Groans emanated from the group.

"How long?"

"Are we going to be late for the competition?"

"Can we get off this bus?"

Sister Murphy held up her hands, "Everything will be fine, we just have to wait for the man to come and fix the bus and then we can be on our way."

"Can we at least get out and walk around? It's hot in here."

"Yea."

"Can we?"

Sister Murphy sighed, "Alright, but stay together, and don't get out of sight of the bus."

The girls emptied the bus, sipping on bottles of water and checking for bars on their cell phones so they could send texts, along with desert selfies, of their latest plight to their friends.

Sabrina Trent trotted down a ditch and ducked behind a pile of boulders. She looked behind her to see the bus and her friends no longer in view. Confident she was alone she took a pack of cigarettes from her purse and lit one.

A voice emanated from behind her, "Oooo, you're gonna get in trouble if Sister Murphy finds out."

Sabrina turned, saw her friend Leann, and exhaled a puff of smoke. "Screw Sister Murphy." Both girls giggled.

"Gimme one," Leann said.

Sabrina offered her friend a cigarette and a light. "Geez, can it get more desolate than this place?" Sabrina flicked away an ash with a cotton-candy pink fingernail.

Leann laughed, "That town we went through didn't even have a mall."

Sabrina rolled her eyes. "G-ross! That's just *stupid*."

To Sabrina, anything she didn't like, or understand, which was a lot, was 'stupid'. It was an epithet she would use right up to the end of her short life.

The girls chatted and smoked, unaware of the six pair of red eyes that watched them.

Leann pointed to a flock of birds circling nearby. "What's up with that?"

Sabrina shrugged, "Maybe something dead, at least that's what I saw on some stupid TV show."

The girls turned at the sound coming from behind the rocks. They backed away as the first Chupacabra came into view.

"Eww, what *is* that?" Sabrina said.

"It's some kind of dog." Leann cocked her head, "Are you lost, doggie?"

The Chupacabra snarled and both girls jumped back.

"We should get back to the bus," Leann said as she backed away.

"Yea." Sabrina flipped her hand at the Chupacabra as she backed away, "Go home! Go home stupid dog."

The Chupacabra advanced on Sabrina and she swung her purse at it, the animal grabbing it between his menacing teeth.

Sabrina tugged on her purse. "Let go!" she screamed. "You stupid dog, let go!"

The animal shook its head, its teeth ripping the fabric of the purse.

"You stupid dog, that's a *Michael Kors*. My mother bought it for me. Let! Go!"

"Sabrina! Leave it, come on," Leann urged.

Both girls ran to the bus, Sabrina fighting with the Chupacabra the entire way. The other five animals now emerged and joined in, stalking the girls as they made their way to the bus and safety.

"Everyone, get in the bus," Leann yelled.

The other girls clambered back onto the bus as Sister Murphy tried to make a head count.

"Sabrina, leave the purse, hurry, get on the bus," Sister Murphy yelled.

Two Chupacabras charged the bus, Sister Murphy closing the door at the last minute and the animals making a 'thud' as they hit the glass door, nearly coming through. The girls in the bus watched as Sabrina, who continued to fight for possession of her designer bag, was now surrounded by Chupacabras.

They banged on the bus windows, yelling, "Sabrina! Sabrina!"

Sabrina backed towards the bus, pulling the bag and its attached Chupacabra. "Stupid dogs. Stupid, stu—"

The girls in the bus screamed and backed away as blood spattered the windows. One girl ran to a clear window. "Oh my Gawd! It's got Sabrina's *Michael Kors* bag." A Chupacabra ran in circles, holding Sabrina's arm in its teeth, the hand with the perfectly manicured pink nails still clutching the bag.

"Jeez! It's got her freakin' arm," Leann said.

Pandemonium broke out in the bus. Sister Murphy did her best to calm the girls but it was of little use.

The six Chupacabras now circled the bus, sniffing the air, snarling, their red eyes watching the movement behind the glass. One animal leaped onto the hood and licked at the windshield, sending the throng screaming to the back of the bus.

Fingernails of every color jabbed at cell phone

buttons as the girls called whoever they could for help.

"Somebody's coming," a girl yelled. Everyone turned to watch a trail of dust grow larger as a vehicle made its way across the high desert scrub.

Rick Steele shifted gears and stepped on the accelerator. He turned to Choo, "Get ready." The Hummer thundered over the desert scrub, sending birds and rabbits scrambling in its wake.

The Chupacabras were now leaping and throwing themselves at the bus, some of the windows showing cracks. The girls huddled in the center while Sister Murphy clutched her crucifix and whispered a prayer, "Blessed Mary, mother of Jesus, save us from these devil hounds."

The frightened young, buxom cheerleaders moved to the windows to watch as the massive vehicle closed on the prowling Chupacabras.

"Deploy," Rick said, as he steered the Hummer for a group of three Chupacabras at the back of the bus.

Choo reached over and flipped a switch and rotating blades folded out from the Hummer's front wheels.

Rick eyed the three beasts that turned to face the oncoming vehicle, their teeth and fangs bared. "You ain't nothin' but a hound dog," Rick murmured. The Hummer hit the Chupacabras head-on, driving directly over one and cutting up the other two with the rotating blades. "A dead hound dog."

Rick jerked hard on the steering wheel, pulling the

Hummer to a skidding stop facing the bus. He looked at Choo, "Ready?"

Choo smiled a toothy grin, "With you, Boss."

The other three Chupacabras slinked around the bus, sniffing at their dead comrades and lowering their heads and growling as they watched Rick and Choo emerge from the Hummer.

Two girls swooned as Rick's muscled arm reached up behind his back and pulled the sawed-off, pump shotgun from its scabbard.

Next to him, Ah Choo reached up with both hands and armed himself with a machete in each hand from the scabbards arranged in X-like fashion on his back.

A flurry of cameras and smart phones blinked on in the bus.

"Did you see that?"

"This is sooo awesome."

"OMG, are they gonna kill those dogs?"

Choo scanned the area, "Three dead, Boss, just these three now."

"Not for long," Rick said, as he locked eyes with one of the Chupacabra. The creature charged, leaping into the air, before a blast from Steele's shotgun threw the beast backward.

The girls in the bus screamed and two dropped their cell phones. Sister Murphy fainted.

Rick pumped his weapon, but Choo shook his head. "I got this, Boss."

The two animals attacked Choo who whirled out of the way, cutting the head off one animal with a single stroke as he turned to face the remaining Chupacabra.

"Finish this up," Rick said, "while I check on the people in the bus."

Choo crossed the machetes in front of him, the blades making an evil sound. "Here, doggie, doggie."

The remaining Chupacabra circled Choo, a feral grin on its muzzle and hair rising along its back. It charged, leaping at Choo's throat.

Choo moved to the side, dropping to one knee and lashing out with both machetes. A primal scream rent the air as the last of the Chupacabras fell to the ground into three pieces.

One of the girls ran forward and pushed the door handle, stepping aside to allow Rick Steele to enter the bus.

"Everyone in here alright?" he asked.

"Sister Murphy, she fainted, but she's better now," came the voice of one of the girls.

"What were those things?" someone asked.

"Dogs," Rick answered, "just some sick, diseased dogs from a nearby ranch. It's all okay now."

He went back outside to Choo. "Bag these up, we need to get samples back to the Professor."

"You got it, Boss."

The earth shook and a noise like a bomb split the air, followed by several smaller explosions. Over the horizon a column of smoke worked its way into the air.

Both Steele and Choo looked at the cloud of smoke.

Rick Steele slipped the shotgun into the scabbard on his back. "I think we're done here."

CHAPTER ONE

THREE YEARS EARLIER, Florida Governor's Mansion

"Did you see this?" Governor Hector Diaz Estéban O'Reilly threw down the morning newspaper. The headline read: 'Tourists Slither Away as Snake Population Grows'.

The Governor's Public Relations aide winced as the paper was slammed onto the conference table. "Sir, it's not that bad, just some reporters looking for—"

"Not that bad? Not that bad? What about these?" The Governor held up a stack of spreadsheets. "Tourism revenues are down fifteen percent. One cruise line is offering 'Snake Free' transport from the airport to their ships. And these TV documentaries about non-indigenous species becoming apex predators, whatever the hell *that* means." He gazed around the room, making eye contact with each person. "People, we have a problem. *I* have an election coming up and if *I'm* out of a job… *You're* out of a job." He sighed and sat in his executive chair at the head of the conference table. "Ideas?"

The assembled group was silent, avoiding eye contact with the Governor or each other.

A voluptuous blonde in a well-fitted gray skirted suit stood. "Sir?" Belinda Drake was the Governor's Chief of Staff, a fierce gate-keeper and a woman with unlimited ambition.

The Governor nodded, "Belinda."

She began to move around the table, the stiletto heels of her expensive designer pumps leaving tracks in the plush carpet. "There *may* be a way. I've made some inquiries. *Discreet* inquiries." She gestured to the closed door, "If I may?"

The Governor looked around the table. "Anyone else have any ideas?" When he received no answers he turned his gaze to Belinda, "You have the floor."

She flashed her trademark charming smile and opened the door, ushering in four men carrying a large box draped in black cloth. Behind them came a tall, bald man, very distinguished looking in an expensive suit.

The men placed the box on the center of the conference and then moved back to the side of the room.

Belinda turned to the conference table, "I'd like to introduce you to Dr. Theerie."

The Governor furrowed his brows, "A doctor of… What? With a University? From the government?"

Dr. Theerie bowed his head and smiled. "A doctor of… Science. And my work is private, but well-funded."

"I see," the Governor rubbed his chin, something he did when considering options. "And you think you have a solution to our unique problem."

"For every problem there is a solution," the doctor said.

There were a few chuckles from the conference table.

The Governor continued, "And your solution would be to…"

Dr. Theerie moved forward and removed the cloth covering the box. It was a large rectangular structure with a closed lid, half-filled with sand and with a three-foot

Burmese python on the surface. The women at the table shrank back in horror.

"More snakes?" The Governor raised his hands, "That's your solution? More *snakes*?"

Dr. Theerie smiled, approached the box and tapped rhythmically on the sides, then stepped away.

The sand at the surface vibrated and a creature began to emerge. It was red and segmented, much as a worm, and its head, if it could be called that, contained tentacles and a mouth-like opening. It seemed to taste the air around it and turned in the direction of the python.

The snake took a defensive position, sensing another animal, unable to determine if it was predator or prey.

The flash of light and crackle of electricity made everyone jump and when they looked again, the creature was pulling a stunned python beneath the sand. Within seconds both disappeared.

Governor O'Reilly was wide-eyed. "What in the hell *is* that thing?"

Dr. Theerie folded his hands, "You have witnessed the awesome power of the Mongolian Death Worm."

"It eats snakes?"

"Yes," Dr. Theerie continued, "snakes, birds, insects... But your problem is snakes. When the Mongolian Death Worm begins to feed on the many python hatchlings, then your *problem* will eventually die off as the reproductive cycle is disrupted."

Mike Rawlins, the Chief of Florida Fish and Game stood. "Governor, I don't think introducing yet another foreign species is the solution. It could mean—"

"And what's *your* solution," Governor O'Reilly snapped, "trap and re-locate? You can see where *that* is getting us." He turned back to Dr. Theerie. "Mongolia, that's desert, right? We've got problems in a swamp."

"The creatures are most adaptable," Dr. Theerie assured.

The Governor rose to study the box; he watched the sand move as below the Mongolian Death Worm consumed its prey. "And you can get more of these... These Death Worm things?"

"They *are* elusive, hard to catch and therefore expensive, but yes."

Governor O'Reilly turned and smiled at Belinda, "You saved my ass. You saved *all* of us. Hell, you saved *Florida*!"

Rawlins attempted another protest, "Sir—"

The Governor held up his hand, "No! *This* is the plan. It's simple and effective." He put his arm around Dr. Theerie. "What could go wrong, huh, Doc? What could go wrong?"

Suggested Reading

If you want to know more about the wonderful world of Cephalopods, I highly recommend the book:

KRAKEN

The Curious, Exciting and Slightly

Disturbing Science of the Squid

by

Wendy Williams

About the Author

Greg Causey is retired from a federal service career and now enjoys life as an author, publisher, guitar player, drummer and would-be ballroom dancer. Greg is an Air Force veteran, serving in the 93rd Bomb Wing, SAC. He lives with his wife, and dance partner, Joan in Ohio.

Greg Causey 2012

www.gregcausey.com

Also by Greg Causey

When a mysterious fog rolls in from the sea, Captain Nick is unable to sail to Tree Island to retrieve the town's annual Christmas tree. Without the tree, the town of Christmas Bay will not be able to celebrate Christmas. Timmy and Sally, with their friend, Sid the Squid, come up with an idea to save the day. Will the little squid be able to help the town and save Christmas?

SID the SQUID Saves Christmas contains thirteen illustrations and a seven page activity section with puzzles, games and coloring for even more squid fun!

SID the SQUID Saves Christmas is also available as an e-book and audio book narrated by Kellie Kamryn. Look for these versions at your favorite on-line retailer.

RICK STEELE: Squid Hunter

1945, Berlin: In the last days of the war SS Major Jürgen Strasser is summoned to the Führerbunker for one last, desperate mission.

Present Day: Antiques dealer, and ex IRA assassin, Patrick Deveraux is caught up in a race to find the answers to a decades-old puzzle. As the body count rises in Berlin, the Obersalzburg, Rothenburg and Hamburg, Patrick enlists the help of a Hamburg Dominatrix and a North Sea fishing boat skipper to find the truth. Their search takes them from the seedy sex clubs of Hamburg's Reeperbahn to Hitler's Eagle's Nest in Bavaria. Who will live, who will die, and who will survive an interrogation in Mistress Hannelore's dungeon?

ISBN Print: 978-1-934446-67-6

ISBN e-Book: 978-1-934446-68-3

Dancing With Natasha takes the reader from "I Can't Dance," to "I'm A Dancing Machine." Greg and co-author Natasha detail the often agonizing, but always rewarding endeavor of learning Ballroom Dance. In this engaging, witty and poignant memoir, Greg and his wife, Joan make the trek to the Arthur Murray Dance Studio in Dayton, Ohio, for a few lessons to better enjoy the professional formal functions they attend. What they find is nothing short of miraculous. In her own exuberant style, Natasha, their Russian instructress, explains how she moves beginners who consider the obligatory grope' on the floor to be dancing, to graceful self-expression. With the foreword written by Barbara Haller, Four-time United States Professional Theatrical Arts champion, and details from other students, instructors, and dance pros, *Dancing With Natasha* gives the reader an uncommon peek into this incredibly popular and exciting endeavor.

ISBN Print: 978-1-934446-00-3
ISBN e-Book: 978-1-934446-14-0

Denizens of the Desert contains photographs from the collection of former Aerospace Maintenance And Regeneration Center (AMARC) employee Danny Causey. Chapters are devoted to aircraft nose art found on B-52, KC-135, A-10 and F-111 aircraft. Additional chapters include photographs of other AMARC aircraft and a chapter on U.S. Navy aircraft at AMARC (photographer Danny Causey was a veteran of the USS Midway).

For most of the aircraft, this was their last landing, the last stop in storied histories. They would be cannibalized for spare parts, or cut up and reclaimed for their metals. A special few might find refuge in museums or displays. And one lone man would walk their ranks, photograph them and bid them a last goodbye.

Photographs by Danny Causey   Edited by Greg Causey
Print: ISBN: 978-193-4446-15-7

High Heels and Scatter Diagrams?

Run Charts and Foreplay?

Quality Sex: The Sensuous Side of Process Improvement takes a unique look at quality and process improvement. The Plan-Do-Check-Act model gets a sultry, sensuous and fun interpretation.

Greg Causey is a member of the American Society for Quality (ASQ) and is a certified Quality Manager and Quality Technician.

Limited personally signed copies available direct from the author at:

greg@romancedivine.com